Advanced Dungeons & Dragons 2nd Edition

Player's Handbook

Rules Supplement

The Complete Book of Humanoids

by Bill Slavicsek

TSR Inc.

Table of Contents

Introduction...4
Kulung's Tale 4
What are Humanoids? 4
Humanoids in Campaigns 5
The Purpose of This Handbook.....................5
A Note About Optional Rules 6

Chapter One: Humanoid Characters 7
Creating Humanoid Characters 7
    Getting Started 7
Generating Ability Scores...............................7
Humanoid Races 8
Groups, Classes, and Kits...............................8
    Multi-Class Characters 8
    Character Class Maximum Levels 8
    Exceeding Level Limits 8
Adding Humanoids to a Campaign 9
    Campaign Model #1.....................................9
    Campaign Model #2.....................................11
    Campaign Model #3.....................................12
    Campaign Model #4.....................................13

Chapter Two: Humanoid Races 15
How to Read the Entries...................................15
    Aarakocra 16
    Alaghi..18
    Beastman 19
    Bugbear...21
    Bullywug, Advanced 22
    Centaur 24
    Fremlin 25
    Giant-kin, Firbolg..27
    Giant-kin, Voadkyn 29
    Gnoll...31
    Gnoll, Flind 32
    Goblin...35
    Hobgoblin..36
    Kobold..38
    Lizard Man 40
    Minotaur 42
    Mongrelman..43
    Ogre, Half-Ogre..46
    Ogre Mage 47
    Orc, Half-Orc...49
    Pixie..51

Satyr 53
Saurial 55
Swanmay 59
Wemic...60

Chapter Three: Humanoid Kits 62
Kit Descriptions 62
Warrior Kits 63
    Tribal Defender 65
    Mine Rowdy..66
    Pit Fighter...67
    Saurial Paladin 69
    Sellsword 70
    Wilderness Protector....................................72
Wizard Kits 73
    Hedge Wizard 74
    Humanoid Scholar 75
    Outlaw Mage 76
Priest Kits...77
    Shaman 78
    Witch Doctor 79
    Oracle...80
    War Priest 81
    Wandering Mystic 82
Rogue Kits 83
    Scavenger...84
    Tramp 85
    Tunnel Rat 86
    Shadow 87
    Humanoid Bard 88

Chapter Four: Humanoid Proficiencies 90
Proficiencies and Specialization 90
Nonweapon Proficiencies................................92
    Acting..92
    Alertness 92
    Animal Noise 92
    Begging 92
    Blind-fighting 92
    Chanting 93
    Cheesemaking...93
    Close-quarter Fighting..................................93
    Craft Instrument 94
    Crowd Working 94
    Danger Sense..94

Table of Contents

Drinking..94
Eating 94
Fast-talking.......................................95
Fortune Telling..................................95
Hiding 95
Information Gathering 96
Intimidation 96
Looting...96
Natural Fighting...............................96
Observation.......................................97
Poetry 97
Voice Mimicry 97
Whistling/Humming 97
Wild Fighting 97
Winemaking 98

Chapter Five: Role-Playing Humanoids ..100
Life as a Humanoid 100
Tribal Life..101
Social and Racial Disadvantages.................101
Humanoid Traits 103
Campaign Complications 105

Chapter Six: Superstitions 107
A Mysterious World.......................107
Superstitions in Game Terms.................107
Using Superstitions in Play.................108
The Superstitions...........................109

Chapter Seven: Arms and Armor..............111
Armor Restrictions..........................111
Weapon Size Restrictions.................111
Weapon Breakage (Optional) 111
Close-quarter Weapons...............111
Special Humanoid Weapons 112

Humanoid Comparison Chart...................115

Humanoid Character Sheets.....................122

INDEX TO TABLES
1: Humanoid Group Limits....................9,120
2: Bonus Levels for Single-Classed
  Humanoids..................................9,120
3: Nonweapon Proficiency Group
  Crossovers 63
4: Nonweapon Proficiencies...................90
5: Personal Superstitions 108
6: Optional Weapon Breakage...................111
7: Weapons......................................114
8: Character Kit Summary 116
9: Average Height and Weight...................116
10: Age..117
11: Aging Effect 117
12: Racial Ability Requirements 118
13: Multi-Class Combinations....................119
14: Thieving Skill Racial Adjustments........118
15: Reincarnation Table................................120
16: Monstrous Traits 121
17: Bestial Habits 121
18: General Superstitions............................121
19: Campaign Complications.....................121

CREDITS

Design: Bill Slavicsek
Editing: Jon Pickens
Black and White Art: Doug Chaffee
Color Art: Doug Chaffee, Sam Rakeland,
Thomas Baxa, Clyde Caldwell
Typography: Tracey Zamagne
Production: Paul Hanchette

TSR, Inc.
POB 756
Lake Geneva
WI 53147
U.S.A.

TSR Ltd.
120 Church End
Cherry Hinton
Cambridge CB1 3LB
United Kingdom

Introduction

Kulung's Tale

I travel the back roads of human civilization, following a quest I do not always understand. Some unseen force, some inner desire, drew me away from my tribe and brought me to the towns and cities of humanity. Does this mean I reject my place as an ogre mage? I do not think so. Instead, I believe I am trying to enhance it.

I wander the edges of human settlements, drawn like an insect to the brightly burning torch of civilization. Like an insect, I cannot turn away from the intense heat. Like an insect, I will be destroyed if I get too close to the flame. I am fascinated, captivated, afraid.

But the fear flows both ways. While I fear the screaming mobs of humans with their swords and clubs and sharp-tipped arrows, they also fear me. To most of them, I am a monster. I look different. I sound different. I pray to different gods. Humans are quick to show fear toward that which is different. And what they fear, they often destroy.

Why did I leave my tribe? The answer is at once simple and complex. I was not like my tribe mates. I rejected the practice of catching and keeping slaves. I followed a path that was closer to good than to evil. I even sought out knowledge and scholarly endeavors while my tribe mates reveled in combat and conquest. In short, I was different, much different, and humanoids are less tolerant of differences than even the humans and demihumans whose lands I now roam.

I live in humanity's shadow, but I am not a shadow of humanity. Indeed, those few humans who I have come to call friend proclaim that I am more human than most of their kind. Sometimes I take this as a compliment, sometimes a foul curse, for I have seen the heights that humanity can reach and I have witnessed the dark depths it can sink to. They are grand, these humans, but they are also desperately dangerous. And the greatest danger lies in the bright center of civilization's flame, for it draws me toward its scrolls and books and epic ballads, where its searing heat can consume me. Perhaps it is better in the shadows, for the darkness offers some small protection from the flame.

Am I a monster? It depends on the point of view. To my own people, I am a weakling, a coward, a failure. To the humans and demihumans who know me, I am a trusted companion, a learned associate and a friend. To those who refuse to see beyond my appearance, I am a foul creature, a hated enemy, a monster. I am all these things and none of them. I am Kulung the Ogre Mage, the Tribeless One, the Searcher.

I am the Humanoid, and I walk the perimeter of humanity's blazing flame.

What are Humanoids?

Every AD&D® game has them. Most often, they are under the control of the DUNGEON MASTER™. When player characters encounter them, they usually appear in the role of villain or opponent. They are the humanoids, monsters that have two arms, two hands, at least two legs, and stand generally upright.

From a distance, within the folds of a hooded cloak, or obscured by deep shadows, humanoids can be mistaken for humans. Only on closer inspection and in the light of day are they immediately seen for what they are. They bear the general shape of humanity, but they have startling — and often times frightening — differences. Some are taller or broader than the average human. Others are smaller, frailer. Many have misshapen features, wicked claws and fangs, thick fur or long, dank hair. Humanity is one race, humanoid races are legion.

Humanoids have their own cultures, societies, morals, values, and attitudes. These vary greatly from the general human experience. They are more than "humans in funny suits," or at least they should be in a well-developed campaign world. The world looks vastly different through the cruel eyes of a minotaur or the bulging eyes of a bullywug. It is these differences that separate the human from the humanoid — and these differences create the greatest challenges and most fun when playing a humanoid character.

Humanoids in Campaigns

Humanoids have been a major part of the AD&D® game from the beginning. Who has not sent his or her favorite character up against a horde of goblins, a dungeon full of hobgoblins and bugbears, or an ogre of monstrous proportions? And yet, over the years, the same character may have received timely help from a flock of screeching aarakocra, been guided to safety by a herd of noble centaurs, or have been given critical information by a beautiful swanmay.

Now it's time for something different. Just as not every thief is a greedy scoundrel and not every warrior is a dim-witted bully, not every humanoid fits the mold that we have come to know over the years. Some decide to leave dungeon and lair behind to take up the life of an adventurer — though these fellows are rare indeed! Not only must such humanoids go against the norms of the very societies they were born into (in most cases), but often they find prejudice and rejection wherever the spirit of adventure leads them. The adventuring humanoid ever struggles to find acceptance and a place to fit in, while taking on the quests his spirit demands. Perhaps the next adventure will bring him to such a place, for it always seems to be just over the next hill and around the next bend.

This is the drama and tension of which good stories are made — and great role-playing game campaigns. By opening a campaign to humanoid player characters, players and Dungeon Masters alike are opening a mysterious box. Ultimately, what's in the box depends on the attitudes of everyone involved. It could contain a wondrous reward of challenge and fun, or it could hold the key to a campaign's destruction. It all depends on how humanoid PCs are used.

This book attempts to show you how to use humanoids in a positive way to add new dimensions to your role-playing experiences. With moderation, planning, and the cooperation of all involved, humanoid PCs can become important parts of ongoing campaigns. But that doesn't mean every player should immediately roll up a humanoid PC. Too many of these characters will spoil a good thing. We suggest no more than one humanoid PC be used in an adventuring group at any given time. If more than one player wants to try his or her hand at running these unique characters, then they should take turns bringing their humanoid PCs into the game. All of this will be discussed detail later in the book.

The Purpose of This Handbook

The Complete Book of Humanoids is designed to provide rules that allow players to create humanoid player characters. In short, to design and role-play their own monsters!

Every player will use this book in a different way, depending upon a number of factors. Long-time players will turn these pages in search of new role-playing challenges. Some gamers will seek out new abilities to increase the power of their characters. Others will look for a way to combine these for a new role-playing game experience. It all depends on a player's interests and experience, the shape of the campaign world in which the adventures are set, and the interest and commitment of the Dungeon Master.

Skilled players seeking new role-playing challenges should read this book carefully. Others can use the table of contents to find areas of special interest to themselves.

At the end of this book, you'll find new humanoid record sheets. These have been designed to help role-play humanoids, while providing room for all the pertinent game material. There is also a sheet for creating new humanoid kits. These sheets may be photocopied for your personal use.

The back of the book has the tables necessary to create and run humanoid characters. These have been gathered here for convenience and ease of use.

If you need it to create, play, or run a humanoid character, then you'll find it in here. In addition to the basics, there are special sections about superstitions, monstrous traits, social and racial disadvantages, personalities, campaign models for introducing humanoid characters into your game, and campaign complications that a Dungeon Master can use to keep a humanoid character in character.

A Note About Optional Rules

This book is full of new rules, humanoid kits, suggestions on role-playing, new proficiencies and spells, and other details concerning the use of humanoids by the players. This information adds to the rules presented in the *Player's Handbook*. However, this is only a supplement to that volume. All of the rules in this book are optional. As a player, you should be prepared to abide by your Dungeon Master's decisions about how to use any of these new rules in the campaign.

Even if your Dungeon Master decides that none of the rules presented here can be used in his campaign, much can be learned in the pages that follow. Humanoids, after all, are a part of every AD&D® campaign world, and to know them better is to know your game world better. The best way to use this book is to create a humanoid character and play it in a game. Without humanoids, there would be no Kaz™ the Minotaur or Dragonbait™ the Saurial or Kulung™ the Ogre Mage.

And without *The Complete Book of Humanoids*, you won't be able to add your own characters to the ballads of the bards and the tales of the storytellers!

Creating Humanoid Characters

This chapter includes the basic information needed to generate a humanoid character. It explains how to roll ability scores, how to choose classes and kits, and gives guidelines on selecting the humanoid's racial type.

Humanoid characters aren't quite the same as the human or demihuman characters you're used to playing. They often have different motivations, different world views, different limitations. Before you decide whether your humanoid character is going to be noble and misunderstood, suspicious and quick to anger, or some other type, you need to generate and record the character's basic statistics.

Getting Started

A collection of humanoid races has been gathered in this chapter. These races have been selected for their playability and plausibility as player characters. You won't find any undead or spirits among them. There are no monsters that have "instant kill" powers. With few exceptions, all of the humanoids range in size from small to large. We've included a tiny humanoid for variety, but none above the large (7' to 12') size.

Each entry includes background information, role-playing suggestions, monstrous traits and superstitions inherent to the race, minimum and maximum ability scores, racial ability adjustments, class restrictions, and level limits. These will be important when you begin generating ability scores and filling out a character sheet.

Take a few moments to look over the selection of humanoid races. Try to find a race that you want to role-play, not just a race that will generate a powerful character. The goal of this book is to show you how to create characters that can be *role-played* powerfully, not how to create all-powerful monster PCs. In fact, the more powerful a humanoid PC is, the harder it

will be for that character to operate in a campaign setting (see Chapter Five: Role-Playing Humanoids for more information).

After you've selected a race and a couple of alternates, discuss your choices with your Dungeon Master. The one you decide to go with should be the one that you are both comfortable with and fits easily into your DM's campaign. You may have to provide your DM with suggestions on integrating your choice into the campaign setting. By working together to come up with clear campaign hooks and explanations for the humanoid PC's presence, you'll be building something you can both live with. In the long run, cooperating on developing the campaign story will be a rewarding experience for both the Dungeon Master and the players.

When choosing a humanoid race to play, keep in mind the following things. You want to choose a humanoid race that you like, because it's no fun playing a character you can't stand. Your selection should spark plenty of ideas for role-playing the character you want to create. If you have no idea how to run or role-play the ape-like alaghi, or you just hate the thought of playing a lizard man, then you should not choose those races. Finally, you want to select a race that will add positive elements to the story you, the other players and the DM are telling through the role-playing game campaign. A disruptive character, like a disruptive player, will spoil the fun for everyone involved.

Generating Ability Scores

After you've selected the humanoid race you want to play, it's time to create a humanoid player character. You can use any of the six dice rolling methods described in the *Player's Handbook*, provided the method is approved by your DM. If you want to generate a specific character class, and your DM approves, use either method V or VI.

Each humanoid race entry in this chapter includes ability score modifiers. These are applied to the numbers you generate when creating a humanoid character of a particular racial type. Each humanoid race has its own set of ability minimums and maximums. No ability score can fall below the minimum or rise above the maximum without magical or divine aid.

If you have your heart set on playing a particular humanoid race and you roll ability scores that are too high or too low, your DM has the option to allow you to use the racial minimum or maximum for that ability score.

Humanoid Races

Every humanoid race has a maximum experience level it can reach in a given class group (see Table 1: Humanoid Level Limits, on page 9). You may want to look this over before deciding which race you want to play.

Each humanoid race has advantages and disadvantages. If the humanoid race you select has a lot of advantages, it will take more experience points to progress in level. Also, many advantages are often balanced by monstrous traits and superstitions, as described in Chapters Five and Six.

Special Note: Except for swanmays, no humanoid can benefit from a *raise dead* spell. As with elves, other methods of reviving a slain humanoid must be used.

Groups, Classes, and Kits

All four major character groups (warrior, wizard, priest, and rogue) can be found among the humanoid races, though not every character group is open to every race. The individual race entries will list the restrictions, if any, which apply. Similarly, the classes within these groups may be off limits to certain humanoid races.

This book also features character kits for the humanoid races. A kit is a specialized role, designed to augment and enhance the character class system. Kits do not replace classes. Every character who uses a kit still belongs to a particular character class. Kits add detail to characters after their class has been selected.

Kits are entirely optional, though they are recommended. Humanoid characters can be created without them, but the kits add detail that might otherwise be missing. Only one humanoid kit is allowed per character.

Multi-Class Characters

Most humanoids can be multi-class characters, though the combinations available to them varies depending upon what race a humanoid is. If you decide to play a multi-class character, read over the benefits and limitations of such characters as outlined in the *Player's Handbook*. As an option, if a character is ineligible to be multi-classed due to low ability scores, and later has the scores raised to the point of eligibility, the DM may allow the character to declare immediately for multi-class status.

Character Class Maximum Levels

The maximum levels humanoids can attain depend upon the character's race, as listed on Table 1. Multi-class characters can attain the maximum level of each group. Single-classed characters with exceptional scores can attain even higher levels, as listed on Table 2. See individual race entries for further information on groups and classes open to humanoids.

Exceeding Level Limits

As an optional rule, DMs may allow humanoid characters to advance to any level, but they must earn two, three or even four times the amount of experience points normally required for each level. This effect is cumulative with other experience point multipliers that a humanoid race might have.

Adding Humanoids to a Campaign

There are any number of ways to introduce humanoid player characters into a campaign. While the method chosen will be determined by you and your Dungeon Master, this section has a few models that might make the process easier. Consider these models as adventure hooks to introduce a newly-created humanoid player character into the action.

Campaign Model #1: "A Friend in Need..."

Bright Mane found himself at the bottom of a deep pit. The wemic, a cross between lion and human just as a centaur is a cross between human and horse, had stumbled into the trap while hunting for food. The pit, which smelled of humans and their strange tools, was deep enough to keep Bright Mane from leaping out, even if he hadn't injured his hind leg in the fall. The sides of the pit were too steep to climb, and he was quickly running out of ideas. Soon, he knew, the humans would come to see what they had caught in their pit. Then his exploration of the world beyond his nation's territory would end — as would his freedom, and perhaps his life.

As twilight stretched across the land, Bright Mane heard the sound of clanking armor approaching. He tensed, tightening his grip on his primitive spear. He would not give up without a fight! That was not the way of a warrior of the pride!

"What have they caught this time?" a gravelly voice asked. Bright Mane looked up to see a dwarf peering down at him. Behind the dwarf was a human, dressed in the polished armor of a paladin.

"Whatever it is, I won't see it taken as slave by those vile predators," the paladin proclaimed. "Let's see if we can extract it before Barrot and his men return ..."

In this campaign model, the human and demihuman PCs who have been operating in the DM's campaign world come to the rescue of the newly-created humanoid PC. Like the

Table 1: Humanoid Level Limits

| Race | Character Group | | | |
	Wr	Wz	Pr	Rg
Aarakocra	11	—	7	11
Alaghi	12	—	11	—
Beastman	12	—	—	10
Bugbear	12	—	8	9
Bullywug	10	—	7	9
Centaur	12	12	14	12
Fremlin	—	10	—	12
Giant-kin, firbolg	12	—	7	—
Giant-kin, voadkyn	11	8	7	10
Gnoll	11	—	9	11
Gnoll, flind	12	—	9	11
Goblin	10	—	9	12
Hobgoblin	11	—	9	12
Kobold	8	—	9	12
Lizard Man	12	—	7	9
Minotaur	12	8	7	10
Mongrelman	10	10	10	12
Ogre	12	—	3	—
Ogre, half-	12*	—	4	—
Ogre mage	9	8	7	8
Orc	10	—	9	11
Orc, half-	10*	—	4	8
Pixie	7	—	—	12
Satyr	11	—	—	11
Saurial, bladeback	9	9	U	9
Saurial, finback	U	9	9	9
Saurial, flyer	9	9	9	U
Saurial, hornhead	9	U	9	9
Swanmay	14	—	12	—
Wemic	12	—	7	10

* See Table 2

Table 2: Bonus Levels for Single-Classed Humanoids

Prime Requisite Score	Total Bonus Levels
Racial Maximum +1	+1 (+1)
Racial Maximum +2	+2 (+4)
Racial Maximum +3	+3 (+7)

Use the parenthetical number if the prime requisite is Strength and if the humanoid is a human crossbreed (half-orc, half-ogre).

lion with a thorn in its paw, the humanoid is in some kind of trouble that only the non-humanoid PCs can save him from. They take on the role of the mouse, who pulls the thorn free and earns the respect and favor of the terrible lion. By saving the humanoid, the other PCs gain a companion — and perhaps even a friend.

Once saved, the humanoid PC forms a bond with his rescuers. He feels he owes them a debt he can never repay, or at least that he owes them a debt which must be paid off through the course of subsequent adventures. Even if the other PCs protest, the humanoid will not be swayed from paying back his debt in whatever way he can think of. He will follow his saviors, protect them, aid them in their quests, and seek to return the great favor that they have bestowed upon him.

Humanoids can be saved from a variety of situations, including angry mobs, other adventurers, town guards, hostile monsters, natural disasters, and even other humanoids. A humanoid PC who has been rescued will be totally devoted to his saviors if he is of the proper alignment and personality. Even the most independent and chaotic humanoids will see the other player characters as companions who will keep them from getting into deadly trouble again.

Campaign Model #2: "...Is a Friend Indeed."

The trolls were closing in on Grellor at last, and the ranger had nowhere else to run to. He had reached the end of the path. Above him was the steep cliff walls of the mountain pass, below him was a dizzying drop into oblivion. His only option was to turn and face the trio of trolls, though this would only delay the inevitable. His sword and tiring muscles were no longer a match for the regenerating monsters.

The trolls appeared from around the bend, first one with drooling jaws and outstretched talons, then another, and another. They moved slowly,

sensing that the chase had ended and wanting to continue the game for a while longer. Grellor swung his sword before him, hoping to keep the monsters at bay. By the look on the lead troll's face, that tactic wasn't going to work. He watched as the vile creature tensed, preparing to leap across the remaining space and sink its claws into his tender, tired flesh.

What happened next was a confused jumble. The lead troll leaped. Grellor screamed and jumped back, plunging over the side of the cliff. He heard another scream over his own, like the cry of a huge bird. "Skree-ya!" it called, and Grellor felt bony hands grasp him. He looked up to see a winged humanoid — an aarakocra, he believed it was called — grab him. While it could not hold his weight and maintain flight, it could slow their fall toward the water below.

"Breeka save human," the aarakocra crowed in broken common as they glided downward. "She have wings enough for both of us ..."

In this model, it is the human or demihuman player characters who are in deadly trouble. While this model works best on an individual level (one human/demihuman PC, one humanoid PC), it can be developed to apply to an entire player character group.

On an individual level, the human and the humanoid form a bond due to the heroic efforts of the humanoid character. This bond can start as one of gratitude and a debt to be repaid, but it often develops into a long-term adventuring companionship or even a close personal friendship between the human in need of help and his humanoid savior.

On a group level, the humanoid character provides the means for adventurers to get out of a terrible jam. She may know a secret passage out of the dungeon, or a hidden pass through goblin territory, or she may even charge into battle to save the adventurers from certain doom. In this way, the entire group owes a debt to the humanoid. They may not all become fast friends with their savior, but they will show a grudging respect and will feel

obligated to her.

Adventurers get into all sorts of situations that they might need to be rescued from. A trap in a dungeon could leave them all unconscious and dying until the humanoid pulls them to safety. Hordes of monsters could be closing in and the adventurers must prepare to fight to the death, when the humanoid shows them a way to escape. Or perhaps the humanoid leads them to a pool of healing, or to a much needed cache of supplies, or even intercedes on behalf of the adventurers to save them from her own people.

Whatever the situation, a humanoid who helps a group of adventurers out of a life-or-death encounter becomes very attached to her charges. She believes that they will always need her help, that if she leaves them to their own devices they will simply wind up back in trouble again — or worse. Because of this, the humanoid decides to accompany them on their adventures. For their part, the adventurers feel

beholden to the humanoid, so they tolerate her presence. As the humanoid shows her resourcefulness and ability to help over and over again, she will become an important part of their group. Perhaps over several gaming sessions, she will even become their friend.

Campaign Model #3: "Hello, Again..."

Freg the Rogue sat staring into the dying campfire, trying not to think about what his beloved Dreeya might return as. The woman warrior was struck down in their escape from the Underdark, and the only option that had been open to Freg was to allow the priest Joun to cast her miracle. Now he could only wait.

"Are you certain you have no idea what form Dreeya will come back in?" Freg asked the cleric for the tenth time since they had finished dinner.

"Reincarnate is not an exact spell," Joun explained again. "She may return as an animal, or

perhaps even as a humanoid."

Freg jabbed a long stick into the fire, producing a burst of sparks. "If you knew Resurrection we wouldn't be sitting here waiting to see ..."

The conversation ended abruptly as a sound broke the stillness beyond the camp. The thief and the priest turned in the direction of the noise, trying to make out shapes in the darkness beyond the fire's glow. They heard it again. Someone or something was approaching the camp.

"Dreeya?" Freg called cautiously. "Dreeya, is that you?"

"Yes, my dearest," a voice called back. It was a feminine voice, but it was also very deep and not quite human. Freg gulped.

A dark shadow reached the edge of the camp, hesitated, then slid into the fire's light. Standing before Freg and Joun, barely able to contain a smile, was a huge, obviously female, bugbear.

"Dreeya has returned," the bugbear said, fixing Freg with a loving look. "Miss me?"

A human or demihuman player character eventually faces a foe that is stronger, tougher, and luckier than he is. On such an occasion, the result is often the untimely death of the player character. Of course, death is not always final for PCs in a campaign. There are a number of methods for rescuing a favorite character from the bony clutches of death. The method which concerns us here is the priest spell, *reincarnate*.

The list of possible incarnations has been expanded to include the humanoid races listed in this book. Now that there are rules for creating and playing humanoid characters, it makes sense to provide this method for turning a dead human or demihuman PC into a live humanoid PC.

This method creates a situation that is unlike the other methods for introducing a humanoid PC into a campaign. While the other methods bring an "uncivilized" humanoid into the company of human and demihuman adventurers, *reincarnate* places the memories and personalities of deceased humans into the body of a human-oid. The character must now cope with life from inside a very different body than he was used to. He must face all of the prejudices directed at that body without the benefit of growing up in the culture it belongs to. A new humanoid character introduced through *reincarnate* may look like a bugbear or satyr, but it has all (or at least most) of the knowledge and understanding of the human character it used to be.

The reincarnated character recalls the greater part of his former life and form. The character class of the new incarnation can be anything the player wants, as long as it fits the rules presented in this book and matches the humanoid race in question.

If a humanoid character is being created using the *reincarnate* spell, it follows these rules: If the character returns as the same class as his previous incarnation, the reincarnated humanoid has half his previous levels and hit points. If the humanoid returns as a new character class, his hit points are half his previous total, but he must begin again at first level.

Campaign Model #4: "All that Glitters..."

The goblin sat across from Valkira and her companions, slurping the mug of wine she had offered it with greedy delight. It drained the contents quickly, licking the last drops from the bottom of the mug. Then it belched loudly, licked again, and finally dropped the empty mug before turning its unusually bright eyes upon Valkira.

"Can you really lead us through the passages beneath the Sunset Mountains?" the warrior woman asked, watching the goblin closely for signs of deception or betrayal.

"Grolip know passages like Grolip know back of foot," the goblin boasted easily. "Grolip lead you — if pay is right."

"We'll pay what we agreed upon," Valkira assured him. "Half now, half on the other side. Plus, if all goes well, we'll give you an additional fifty as a bonus."

The goblin's eyes widened at the promise, and his fangs protruded in a lopsided grin. "For that, Grolip even help you carry your treasure!"

"That's okay," Valkira said quickly. "Just lead us through the passages safely."

"You safe with Grolip," the goblin nodded eagerly. "Grolip know way …"

In this campaign model, the adventurers hire the services of a humanoid for a particular adventure and wind up getting a life-long companion. Perhaps they aren't able to pay him right away and he decides to hang around until the money becomes available. Maybe circumstances turn employers and employee into partners or even friends. In most cases, what starts as an honest business arrangement evolves into something more. The humanoid might be in it for the money in the beginning, but circumstances often turn business associates into boon companions — especially in the violent, dangerous realms where adventurers tend to roam.

Humanoids can be hired for any number of jobs, including hired muscle, as guides or interpreters, and even for some particular skill or knowledge the humanoid might have. Those humanoids who make good player characters often hire themselves out in order to earn money until they can hook up with an adventuring party that will accept them. Often, the only legal employment a humanoid can find is as a hireling to adventurers.

During the course of employment, the humanoid will come to enjoy the company of the adventurers, perhaps even hooking onto one particular character as a friend. He will demonstrate his own abilities and worth to the party as the adventure progresses, and even prove his loyalty on more than one occasion. When the time comes to collect his pay and move on, the humanoid will make excuses to stay. He may admit to wanting to stay out of friendship, or he may pretend that only the promise of more wealth keeps him around. In either case, the party gains the skills of the humanoid character, and the humanoid gains the companionship of the adventurers.

Basic information on humanoid races can be found in the various *Monstrous Compendium*™ sets. As the humanoids who become player characters are rare examples of their races, the information that follows (except for rules material) is intended only as a guideline. What may be true of one member of a humanoid race may not be true of another. Individual alignments can vary, as can backgrounds, goals, and motivations.

How to Read the Entries

Each entry for a humanoid character type includes the following elements:

Ability Score Adjustments. These modify the ability scores when the humanoid is selected. They are added to or subtracted from the scores rolled. The adjusted ability score is entered on your character sheet.

Ability Score Range. This lists the minimum and maximum ability scores a humanoid character can have when first created. Scores that exceed the maximum or fail to meet the minimum can be adjusted down or up to the limit only if the DM allows it; otherwise a different character type must be chosen.

Of course, over time a character's ability scores may change. Only at the time of a character's creation must the minimums and maximums be adhered to.

Note that the maximum *Charisma* score is that perceived by other races. A rolled score higher than this has its full effect on members of the character's own race.

Class Restrictions and Level Limits. Which classes are open to the humanoid and how far the character can advance can be found here.

Multiclass options are listed on page 119. In general, a humanoid must have scores of 14 in the prime requisites of both classes to become a multiclass character.

Hit Dice. Humanoid hit dice depend on the class selected. Any special hit point bonus the humanoid receives is listed here.

Alignment. The race's typical alignment is listed here. The range of PC options is usually more extensive.

Natural Armor Class. Some humanoid races have a natural armor class which provides protection without the benefit of artificial armor. This rating does not include Dexterity bonuses or penalties.

Generally, protection rated at less than or equal to the natural armor class will provide +1 AC protection. Thus, a lizard man (with a natural armor class of 5) wearing studded leather armor is AC 4. Should the character somehow contrive to have a set of plate mail constructed, it would give him a base AC 3.

Background. This describes the humanoid in general terms, painting a broad picture of the particular race and its members. The player should also detail the character's background in order to fully integrate the character into the campaign. Such additional details are subject to the approval of the DM.

Languages. This section lists the languages which are commonly spoken by the members of a particular race. A character always speaks his native language. Additional languages may be known. It is highly recommended that all humanoid PCs understand common.

If the DM uses the nonweapon proficiency system, additional languages require proficiency slots. A humanoid character's native language does not require a slot. Additional languages do (see Chapter Four: Humanoid Proficiencies). If the DM is not using the nonweapon proficiency system, then the humanoid characters know a specific number of additional languages based upon their Intelligence scores (see *Player's Handbook*).

Role-Playing Suggestions. This gives a few suggestions on how to role-play a member of this particular race. The players can use these suggestions or ignore them as they see fit.

Special Advantages. This lists any special advantages benefitting the members of a particular humanoid race.

Special Disadvantages. This lists any special disadvantages that hinder the humanoid.

Monstrous Traits. These are the typical traits exhibited by the members of this race. Such traits help distinguish one humanoid race from another.

Optionally, the DM may require humanoid characters to take additional monstrous traits, depending on the number of special advantages the humanoid has (see Chapter Five).

Superstitions (Optional). This section lists sample superstitions that best fit a particular humanoid race.

Proficiencies. The entries for weapon and nonweapon proficiencies list each humanoid race's initial selections. Unless the DM approves another proficiency, or a special kit is taken, PCs of a particular humanoid race must select their initial proficiencies from their lists (proficiencies available through humanoid kits are listed in Chapter Three). When a new proficiency slot is gained by level advancement, the new proficiency can be selected from any weapon or group available to the kit or character class.

Aarakocra

Ability Score Adjustments. The initial ability scores are modified by a +1 bonus to Dexterity, and a –1 penalty to Strength and Constitution.

Ability Score Range

Ability	Minimum	Maximum
Strength	3	16
Dexterity	8	18
Constitution	6	16
Intelligence	3	18
Wisdom	3	17
Charisma	3	18

Class Restrictions

Class	Maximum Level
Warrior	
Fighter	11
Ranger	—
Paladin	—
Wizard	
Mage	—
Illusionist	—
Priest	
Cleric	—
Druid	—
Shaman	7
Witch Doctor	—
Rogue	
Thief	11
Bard	—

Hit Dice. Player character aarakocra receive hit dice by class.

Alignment. Aarakocra tend toward neutral good. PC aarakocra may be of any alignment.

Natural Armor Class. 7.

Background. Aarakocra are a race of intelligent bird-men that live among the highest mountain peaks. The average aarakocra stands

about five feet tall and has a wing span of twenty feet. Halfway along the edge of each wing is a hand with three human-sized fingers and an opposable thumb. An elongated fourth finger extends the length of the wing and locks in place during flight.

The hands cannot grasp while flying, but are nearly as useful as human hands when an aarakocra is perched and its wings folded back. Their powerful legs end in four sharp talons that can unlock and fold back to reveal another pair of functional hands.

These humanoids have hollow, fragile bones. Their faces combine the features of both parrots and eagles. They have gray-black beaks and black eyes. Plumage color varies, but males generally have red, orange, and yellow coloration, while females tend toward brown and gray.

Aarakocra live in small tribes which control hunting territories and share a communal nest. The eldest male serves as leader, the second oldest as shaman.

Languages. Aarakocra, giant eagle, common.

Role-Playing Suggestions. Aarakocra are reluctant to engage in ground or grappling combat because of their fragile bones. They love gems and other shiny objects. Their religious ceremonies are simple affairs involving whistled hymns. Sunset on the first day of each new month is of religious significance.

These bird-men enjoy peace and solitude. They love their freedom, and are extremely claustrophobic. Most of them will not enter a cave, building, or other enclosed area without a very good reason.

Aarakocra PC adventurers must have clear motivations. Some leave on a quest to aid their people, others because they do not fit in with the rest of their tribe.

Aarakocra who learn common intersperse the language with their native bird-like sounds. Caws, screeches, and whistles punctuate their broken sentences in typical bird-like fashion (like a parrot mimics human speech).

Aarakocra fighters prefer heavy fletched javelins when they must go to battle. An aarakocra can carry up to six javelins in individual sheaths strapped to his chest. While flying, he can clutch a javelin in each of his lower hands, throwing them or stabbing opponents as necessary. Aarakocra who have left their home territory and traveled to more civilized lands will sometimes wear pieces of studded leather armor to provide additional protection. They never carry shields.

Some tribes of aarakocra carry a special weapon, called a *flight lance*. See Chapter Seven: Arms and Armor, for more details.

Special Advantages. The bird-men have the ability to fly, with a movement speed of 36 and a maneuverability class of C.

Aarakocra talons cause 1-3 points of damage and can strike twice in a round. Their beaks also cause 1-3 points of damage. They receive no attack penalties for aerial missile fire. When using two javelins, an aarakocra can make a diving attack. They must dive at least 200 feet to use this special attack. The attacks are usually accompanied by a blood-curdling shriek, gain a +4 bonus to the attack rolls, and cause double damage.

An aarakocra shaman of 7th level can, with four other aarakocra, summon a friendly air elemental in three rounds of chanting and aerial dancing. It will perform favors, although it will not endanger its life for them.

Special Disadvantages. Aarakocra are very claustrophobic. Those who engage in combat in enclosed areas (buildings, dungeons, etc.) receive a -3 penalty to their attack rolls.

Monstrous Traits. Monstrous speech; aarakocra make bird sounds when speaking, even if talking in the common tongue.

Superstitions. Fear of enclosed spaces.

Weapon Proficiencies: Dagger, dart, javelin, *flight lance* (if available).

Nonweapon Proficiencies: Alertness, animal noise, danger sense, direction sense, hunting, survival (mountains), weather sense, weaving.

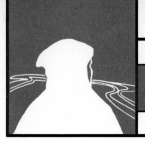

Alaghi

Ability Score Adjustments. The initial ability scores are modified by a +2 bonus to Strength and a –2 penalty to Intelligence.

Ability Score Range

Ability	Minimum	Maximum
Strength	12	19
Dexterity	3	17
Constitution	12	18
Intelligence	3	16
Wisdom	3	16
Charisma	3	16

Class Restrictions

Class	Maximum Level
Warrior	
Fighter	12
Ranger	—
Paladin	—
Wizard	
Mage	—
Illusionist	—
Priest	
Cleric	—
Druid	11*
Shaman	—
Witch Doctor	—
Rogue	
Thief	—
Bard	—

* Int 15+, Wis 12+, Cha 15+ alignment neutral good.

Hit Dice. Player character alaghi receive hit dice by class. In addition, they receive 9 bonus hit points at first level.

Alignment. Alaghi tend toward true neutral alignment. PC alaghi may be of any alignment. Alaghi druids are neutral good.

Natural Armor Class. 4.

Background. Alaghi, distant relations to yeti, are forest-dwelling humanoids. They have bar-

rel chests, short necks, and wide, flat heads. Their short legs are thick, their hands and feet are large, and their hair is thick: blond, reddish brown, or charcoal gray. They stand about 6 feet tall and weigh over 300 pounds.

Most alaghi live as semi-nomadic hunter-gatherers. Sedentary alaghi set up communities of crude huts or large cave complexes. Alaghi communities are generally mistrusted, though some neighbors will trade manufactured goods for pelts, game, and ore. The rarest alaghi are philosophical hermits that are neutral good and have druidic abilities.

The primitive alaghi fashion crude stone knives, hand axes, and tools, as well as simple wooden javelins. A favorite tactic employed by the alaghi is to hurl missile weapons from hiding, ambushing their opponents.

Languages. Alaghi, common.

Role-Playing Suggestions. These forest dwellers tend to be shy and peaceful. The hermitic alaghi are curious and helpful to those in need. They love riddles and games of strategy, often seeking competition from willing humans and demihumans. They especially enjoy a good game of chess.

Players should pick the alaghi character's

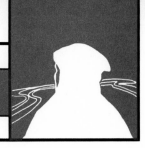

background — nomadic, hermitic, or sedentary. Most will probably be nomadic, traveling in search of adventure as their less heroic kin seek game and wild plants. Nomadic alaghi do not necessarily live in harmony with nature, but they respect it and know how to use it without destroying it. Sedentary alaghi are like primitive humans, often greedy and raiding to survive. Hermitic alaghi live in harmony with nature, usually serving as druids and enjoying friendly relations with their woodland neighbors.

An alaghi deciding to become an adventurer might leave home for a variety of reasons. A nomad leaves its group to seek knowledge, treasure, or adventure. A sedentary alaghi grows tired of community life and again takes up the life of a nomad, eventually hooking up with a group of adventurers and finding a new and exciting activity. A hermitic alaghi may decide to give up a life of solitude for some grand cause — one that usually involves concerns of nature and druidic lore.

Special Advantages. The alaghi's huge fists can inflict 2d6 points of damage. Alaghi can *move silently* as per the thief ability, and they can *hide in natural surroundings*. At 1st level, the base scores are 40% and 35% respectively. Each time an experience level is gained, the alaghi receives another 5% in each skill.

Special Disadvantages. Alaghi take damage as large creatures.

Monstrous Traits. Fearsome appearance, punctuate sentences with hisses, hoots, and grunts. Sedentary alaghi must suppress the urge to slay and eat any non-alaghi they meet.

Superstitions. Fear things which appear to them as unnatural, including wizard spells, undead creatures, and metal arms and armor.

Weapon Proficiencies: Club, hand axe, javelin, knife (all stone weapons).

Nonweapon Proficiencies: Animal lore, animal noise, direction sense, eating, endurance, gaming, hiding, hunting, intimidation, natural fighting, survival (forest).

Beastman

Ability Score Adjustments. The initial ability scores are modified by a +2 bonus to Dexterity, and a penalty of –2 to Charisma.

Ability Score Range

Ability	Minimum	Maximum
Strength	6	18/50
Dexterity	6	18
Constitution	6	16
Intelligence	3	18
Wisdom	3	18
Charisma	3	16

Class Restrictions

Class	Maximum Level
Warrior	
Fighter	10
Ranger	12
Paladin	—
Wizard	
Mage	—
Illusionist	—
Priest	
Cleric	—
Druid	—
Shaman	—
Witch Doctor	—
Rogue	
Thief	10
Bard	—

Hit Dice. Player character beastmen receive hit dice by class.

Alignment. Beastmen tend toward neutral (good) alignment. PC beastmen may be of any alignment.

Natural Armor Class. 8.

Background. Beastmen are short, slender humanoids with a fine layer of dark green or olive colored fur covering their bodies. An inner coat of coarse black fur lies beneath this, which gives them a natural camouflage ability.

Beastmen can instinctively create patterns of stripes or spots across their bodies. The coloration helps them blend in with shadows of the forests from which they hail.

In their native forests, beastmen are dangerous hunters and adversaries. However, they seek to avoid combat and even contact with others unless they must defend themselves or their tribes. They are experts with spears, stone axes and knives, bolas, nets, and blowguns. Some beastmen know how to create a special poison for their blow gun darts. Those who fail a saving throw vs. poison at a +4 bonus die in 2d4 rounds. The toxin can only be prepared in the wild and with the proper ingredients.

Beastman culture is self-sustaining and it does not discriminate against either sex. The average beastman has no need or desire to trade or interact with other races. Of course, beastmen PCs are not of average stock. They possess a healthy curiosity to learn and see new things, though they still hold their own culture to be the superior one.

Languages. Beastmen, common.

Role-Playing Suggestions. Beastmen seldom wear clothing or ornamentation as it interferes with their natural camouflage ability and with the use of their language.

As the beastman language involves spoken words, hand and body gestures, and even the shifting of fur patterns, all other languages they may learn are considered simplistic and primitive. This gives beastmen a natural feeling of superiority over other races.

In the wild, beastmen take on leadership roles depending upon the circumstances. The best qualified takes charge as needed. When working with non-beastmen, they try to continue this honored tradition, usually to the chagrin of their companions.

Special Advantages. Beastmen can make themselves undetected in forest settings, able to hide with 90% chance of success. Opponents who are not aware of the beastman's presence suffer a -6 penalty to their surprise rolls.

Beastmen do not believe in magic, ghosts, spirits, or the supernatural. Only those things which can be seen, touched, tasted, smelled and heard exist. Beastmen are not hindered by superstitions.

A beastman who is proficient in herbalism can expend a proficiency slot to develop the ability to make beastman blowgun poison.

Special Disadvantages. By nature, beastmen are nonmagical. They have 80% magic resistance, even to beneficial effects. They cannot use magical items except for magical weapons, and cannot themselves initiate any special magical functions of such weapons.

Monstrous Traits. Appearance, tendency to roar when completing a hunt.

Superstitions. None.

Weapon Proficiencies: Bola, blowgun, hand axe, knife (stone or wooden weapons).

Nonweapon Proficiencies: Alertness, animal lore, animal noise, cooking, fire-building, fishing, hiding, hunting, rope use, set snares, survival (forest), tracking, wild fighting.

Bugbear

Ability Score Adjustments. The initial ability scores are modified by a +1 bonus to Strength and a –1 penalty to Intelligence and Charisma.

Ability Score Range

Ability	Minimum	Maximum
Strength	8	18
Dexterity	8	17
Constitution	8	18
Intelligence	3	16
Wisdom	3	18
Charisma	3	14

Class Restrictions

Class	Maximum Level
Warrior	
Fighter	12
Ranger	—
Paladin	—
Wizard	
Mage	—
Illusionist	—
Priest	
Cleric	8
Druid	—
Shaman	7
Witch Doctor	7
Rogue	
Thief	9
Bard	—

Hit Dice. Player character bugbears receive hit dice by class. In addition they receive 3 bonus hit points at first level.

Alignment. Bugbears tend toward chaotic evil. PC bugbears may be of any alignment, usually neutral (in rare cases good).

Natural Armor Class. 10.

Background. Bugbears are giant, hairy relatives of goblins. They are large, standing about seven feet tall, with muscular frames and the look of true carnivores. They have light yellow to yellow brown hides, with thick coarse hair that ranges in color from brown to brick red. Bestial eyes of greenish white with red pupils stare out from savage faces. Wedge-shaped ears rise from the top of their heads, and their mouths are full of long sharp fangs.

Bugbears have exceptional sight and hearing, and they move with amazing stealth. They live in caves and underground lairs. Bugbear females are not given the same opportunities and privileges as the males, and a good number of adventurer bugbears are females looking for better lives.

These large humanoids live by plundering and ambush. They sometimes take slaves, and are often cruel and mean-spirited. They are excellent hunters. They eat anything they kill, including humans and humanoids smaller than themselves. Some adventuring bugbears leave their lairs because they cannot stand to eat intelligent creatures.

A bugbear tribe will have shamans or witch doctors of up to 7th level, but not both.

Languages. Bugbear, goblin, hobgoblin, common.

Role-Playing Suggestions. Bugbears speak a foul sounding language punctuated by gestures, grunts, and snarls. They even use these bestial habits when talking in common, making other races doubt their intelligence.

Even the bravest bugbear PC has trouble breaking away from its tribe. They prefer to ambush their foes rather than attack head on. If outnumbered or overmatched, most will retreat to fight another day.

Adventuring bugbears remain territorial even after they leave their lairs. They mentally mark out territory wherever they go, even when traveling. Anything which comes into this space becomes their property (at least in their own minds), or the property of their new tribe (their PC companions). They are natural bullies, forcing their wills on weaker companions. They are an opportunistic race, prone to

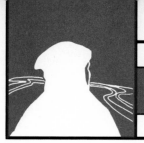

temper tantrums and violent outbursts.

Bugbears enjoy wine and strong ale — often to excess. They are stubborn by nature, finding it difficult to negotiate or compromise. Greed courses through their bodies like blood, and even the most noble bugbear covets glittery, shiny objects and weapons.

Special Advantages. Bugbears have infravision to 60 feet. Their stealth gives opponents a –3 penalty to their surprise rolls.

Special Disadvantages. Bugbears take damage as large creatures.

Monstrous Traits. Monstrous appearance, snarling language, long sharp claws.

Superstitions. Always watchful for omens from the gods; afraid of lightning and violent weather changes; seek to keep on the good side of Skiggaret, the bugbear god of fear.

Weapon Proficiencies: Throwing (footman's) mace, *goblin stick,* hand axe, morning star (*great club*), spear, warhammer.

Nonweapon Proficiencies: Close-quarter fighting, drinking, eating, hunting, intimidation, looting, natural fighting, wild fighting.

Bullywug, Advanced

Ability Score Adjustments. The initial ability scores are modified by a +1 bonus to Dexterity and a –1 penalty to Intelligence and Charisma.

Ability Score Range

Ability	Minimum	Maximum
Strength	6	18/75
Dexterity	4	18
Constitution	6	18
Intelligence	3	14
Wisdom	6	16
Charisma	3	14

Class Restrictions

Class	Maximum Level
Warrior	
Fighter	10
Ranger	—
Paladin	—
Wizard	
Mage	—
Illusionist	—
Priest	
Cleric	—
Druid	—
Shaman	7
Witch Doctor	—
Rogue	
Thief	9
Bard	—

Hit Dice. Player character bullywugs receive hit dice by class.

Alignment. Bullywugs tend toward chaotic evil. PC bullywugs may be of any alignment, but most are neutral or (rarely) good.

Natural Armor Class. 6.

Background. Bullywugs are bipedal frog-like amphibians inhabiting swamps, marshes, and other dank locations. They are covered with a smooth, mottled olive green hide that gives

them a natural protection. They have the faces of enormous frogs, characterized by wide mouths and bulging eyes. Like frogs, their hands and feet are webbed. They wear no clothing, but do make use of crude armor, weapons, and shields.

Bullywugs have learned to cooperate with each other in order to survive and to work together when hunting. They are skilled hunters and fishermen, and can use and build snares and nets.

These frog-men grow up in a savage society. Males are dominant, as females are looked upon as nothing more than egg bearers. Only leaders and their god are shown any kind of respect. Bullywug shamans can advance as high as 7th level, and will always be male.

Bullywugs need to keep their skin moist, which is why they favor swamps and marshes. They love treasure, even if the regular benefits of wealth are lost on their society. Coins, jewels and magical items are hoarded whenever they can be found.

The average bullywug does not display the greed or lust for power seen in other chaotic races. They rarely fight among themselves, except when a leader grows too old or when the smaller, more savage bullywugs meet their larger, more advanced cousins. Bullywugs tend to harm their environment, often hunting and fishing an area until its natural resources are depleted. Most hate humans, attacking them on sight.

Languages. Bullywug, common.

Role-Playing Suggestions. Bullywug PCs are assumed to be the larger, more intelligent (advanced) bullywugs. These range in size from 6 to 7 feet, and are broader than their smaller relatives. They are more aggressive, better organized, and better equipped than the normal bullywugs.

Often it is the females who decide to leave the lair and take up the life of an adventurer, for the opportunities in their own society are extremely limited. While bullywug PCs tend to

remain chaotic, they sometimes shed their evil natures as they try to find a place for themselves in the outside world.

Of course, as most other humans and humanoids fear and detest bullywugs, life for adventurer bullywugs is difficult and dangerous. The successful ones will learn to depend on and cooperate with whatever adventuring group they can latch onto, for their survival depends on cooperation.

Adventuring bullywug shamans often take up service with a new god, for they are usually fleeing from the wrath of the chaotic evil deity of their race.

Special Advantages. Bullywugs have *chameleon* abilities that make them 75% undetectable in natural surroundings. This lets them ambush opponents, whose surprise rolls receive a –2 penalty (–6 if attacked by hop).

Bullywugs employ a *hop attack* which can carry them up to 30 feet forward and 15 feet upward. A hop attack gives them a +1 bonus to their attack rolls. If they are using impaling weapons, these cause double damage.

Bullywugs receive swimming as a bonus proficiency.

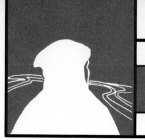

Special Disadvantages. Bullywugs must wet their entire bodies three times a day (at least a waterskin full of water is required). If they are unable to find moisture, they begin to lose Constitution at a rate of 2 points per missed bath. If their Constitution falls to zero, they die from dehydration.

Monstrous Traits. Appearance, chaotic tendencies, webbed hands and feet.

Superstitions. Bullywugs fear dry heat and areas that have little standing water.

Weapon Proficiencies: Club, dagger, short sword, spear, trident.

Nonweapon Proficiencies: Direction sense, fishing, hunting, survival (swamp), weather sense, wild fighting.

Centaur

Ability Score Adjustments. The initial ability scores are modified by a +1 bonus to Constitution and Wisdom, and a –2 penalty to Dexterity.

Ability Score Range

Ability	Minimum	Maximum
Strength	11	18
Dexterity	3	16
Constitution	11	18
Intelligence	3	16
Wisdom	4	18
Charisma	3	18

Class Restrictions

Class	Maximum Level
Warrior	
Fighter	12
Ranger	10
Paladin	—
Wizard	
Mage	12
Illusionist	—
Priest	
Cleric	—
Druid	14
Shaman	7
Witch Doctor	—
Rogue	
Thief	—
Bard	12

Hit Dice. Player character centaurs receive hit dice by class. In addition they receive 4 bonus hit points at first level.

Alignment. Centaurs tend toward neutral or chaotic good. PC centaurs may be any alignment, but are usually neutral or chaotic good.

Natural Armor Class. 5.

Background. Centaurs have the upper torso, arms and head of a human, and the lower body of a horse. These woodland beings are sociable creatures, living in family groups organized into larger tribes. Tribes survive through hunting, foraging, fishing, agriculture and trade. They tend to shun humans, but often trade with elves for food and wine.

Centaurs welcome elves into their areas, sometimes even sharing territory with them. Humans and dwarves receive polite invitations to leave, while halflings and gnomes are usually tolerated.

Centaurs mate for life, and the males clearly have the dominant role in their society. They are pastoral beings who can be violent when the need arises. They live in harmony with nature and know how to conserve resources. They keep things in balance, planting a tree for every one they chop down and taking only what the environment can easily give.

These woodland creatures use a variety of weapons, including oaken clubs, composite bows and medium horse lances. Some carry shields, and a few wear special centaur armor.

Languages. Centaur, elvish, common.

Role-Playing Suggestions. Centaur player characters are either young stallions and mares who have not yet found their life mates, or

widows and widowers who have lost their mates and taken up a life of adventure in order to ease their pain. They are a strong, proud race, easily offended and impulsive.

Centaurs live in balance. They must eat a lot to power their great bodies, and have been known to over-indulge when it comes to wine and ale. Under the influence of alcohol, centaurs display rowdy, boorish, and aggressive behavior.

Those centaurs deciding to explore the world as adventurers usually do so to satisfy an innate curiosity and wanderlust that sometimes becomes a compulsion. They make excellent companions, good fighters, and hardy travelers. While they might sometimes offer a two-legged companion a ride, centaurs do not consider themselves pack animals or sources of transportation. In fact, they often become insulted if such a role is suggested. They also do not tolerate horse jokes, though otherwise they have good senses of humor.

Special Advantages. Centaurs can make three melee attacks in a round: once with their weapons and twice with their front hooves. Hooves cause 1-6 points of damage each.

Centaurs armed with lances can charge for double damage, but cannot attack with their hooves in that same round.

Special Disadvantages. Centaurs take damage as large creatures. They have difficulty negotiating underground settings.

Monstrous Traits. Appearance.

Superstitions. Fear of dragons and giants, see omens and portents in nature.

Weapon Proficiencies: Composite long bow, medium horse lance, *great club.*

Nonweapon Proficiencies: Animal lore, agriculture, animal noise, armorer, artistic ability, bowyer/fletcher, brewing, drinking, eating, fishing, hunting, leatherworking, natural fighting, running, set snares, survival (forests), tracking, weaving, winemaking.

Fremlin

Ability Score Adjustments. The initial ability scores are modified by a +2 bonus to Dexterity, a +1 bonus to Intelligence, and a −3 penalty to Strength.

Ability Score Range

Ability	Minimum	Maximum
Strength	2	11
Dexterity	8	18
Constitution	4	13
Intelligence	6	18
Wisdom	3	16
Charisma	3	18

Class Restrictions

Class	Maximum Level
Warrior	
Fighter	—
Ranger	—
Paladin	—
Wizard	
Mage	10
Illusionist	10

Priest	
Cleric	—
Druid	—
Shaman	—
Witch Doctor	—
Rogue	
Thief	12
Bard	—

Hit Dice. Player character fremlins receive hit dice by class.

Alignment. Fremlins tend toward chaotic neutral. PC fremlins may be of any alignment, but are usually chaotic neutral.

Natural Armor Class. 6.

Background. Fremlins are friendly, mostly harmless gremlins. Like other gremlins, they are small, winged goblinoids, only growing to about a foot in height. However, fremlins tend to be plump and slate colored.

Sometimes fremlins, like their gremlin cousins, are mistaken for imps. While this makes gremlins very angry, it causes fremlins to fall into hysterical fits of laughter. They have large, pointed ears, bat-like wings that give them the power of flight, and an innate immunity to non-magical weapons.

Fremlins shun clothing and ornamentation, believing that they should never hide the wonderful bodies they were born with. They refuse to use weapons, and are generally worthless in combat.

These magical creatures live to have fun, usually at the expense of others. They love to play practical jokes, though their humor tends to be less harmful than that of their gremlin cousins.

Languages. Gremlin (includes fremlin and galltrit), common.

Role-Playing Suggestions. Fremlins are friendly gremlins who tend to be quite harmless. These plump magical creatures are usually whining and lazy, complaining about the least thing and always seeking a way out of real work.

Fremlin player characters are tolerable com-

panions. They usually hook up with a character who befriends them or does something to earn their attention. Those they like receive companionship, those they dislike become the targets of their mischievous pranks.

Fremlins will stick with an adventuring party for a time, remaining as long as they are kept fed and entertained. While they have some useful skills and abilities, fremlin PCs are usually played for comic relief. They seldom assist in combat, and often they wind up hindering the efforts of their companions by giving away hiding locations or making other "innocent" blunders.

These magical creatures are cowards, fleeing at the first sign of trouble. They can be annoying, obnoxious, and easily insulted. Often they will disappear for a time, returning just when the rest of their party believes them to be gone for good. Apologies sometimes bring them back earlier, but usually they stay away until they forget whatever it is that made them mad or depressed in the first place.

Special Advantages. Fremlins are immune to attacks made with normal weapons. Opponents need a +1 weapon or better to hit them.

Fremlins can fly, with a movement speed of 12 and a maneuverability class of B.

Although fremlins rarely fight, they can use tiny weapons specially scaled to their size. Such weapons must be specially made and inflict about one-third normal damage.

Special Disadvantages. None.

Monstrous Traits. Appearance, size.

Superstitions. Fremlins are afraid of almost everything.

Weapon Proficiencies: Dagger, *pixie sword,* other weapons scaled for their size.

Nonweapon Proficiencies: Begging, danger sense, drinking, eating, fortune telling, gaming, hiding, reading/writing, set snares, spellcraft.

Giant-kin, Firbolg

Ability Score Adjustments. The initial ability scores are modified by a +2 bonus to Strength and a –2 penalty to Charisma.

Ability Score Range

Ability	Minimum	Maximum
Strength	14	19
Dexterity	8	15
Constitution	12	18
Intelligence	8	18
Wisdom	8	18
Charisma	3	14

Class Restrictions

Class	Maximum Level
Warrior	
Fighter	12
Ranger	—
Paladin	—
Wizard	
Mage	—
Illusionist	—
Priest	
Cleric	—
Druid	—
Shaman	7
Witch Doctor	—
Rogue	
Thief	—
Bard	—

Hit Dice. Player character firbolgs receive hit dice by class. In addition they receive 13 bonus hit points at first level.

Alignment. Firbolgs tend toward neutral or chaotic good. PC firbolgs may be of any alignment, but are usually chaotic good.

Natural Armor Class. 3.

Background. Firbolgs are the most powerful of the giant-kin. They look like normal humans who have grown to a height of 10½ feet tall and weigh over 800 pounds. Stylish firbolgs wear

their hair long and grow long, thick beards. Their pink skin is very dense and thick, giving them a low natural armor class. They have smooth voices of deep bass and thick, rolling consonants.

These great giant-kin live in remote forests and hills. They distrust most other civilized races and tend to avoid them whenever possible. They get along with druids and faerie creatures, including elves. They do not attack or kill without reason, but they love to engage in pranks which relieve strangers of their valuables.

They have close-knit communities centered around the family or clan. Clans exist as gatherers or nomads, coming together at least once a year with other clans to celebrate or make important decisions.

Firbolgs live off the land, but they also live in harmony with it. They trade their great strength for food with other peaceful folk, supplementing their diet by gathering and hunting. Few monsters bother firbolgs, and they avoid true giants other than storm giants. They refuse to allow other giant-kin to roam their territories.

Languages. Firbolg, common, storm giant.

Role-Playing Suggestions. Firbolgs are extremely confident and quite fearless in most instances. They are a cautious and crafty race, and over the years they have learned to distrust and fear humans and demihumans. They are not overly aggressive, preferring to avoid encounters through hiding and deception. When forced to fight, they employ grand strategies which utilize the terrain and situation around them to best effect. They are taught to operate as a group, not as individuals, and they will carry this trait with them when they take up with adventuring groups.

Firbolg PCs usually adventure to gain knowledge. They are especially interested in increasing their understanding of magic or their collection of treasure. They do not ask for much from their companions, nor do they

expect to give much beyond what is fair.

Firbolgs can use any large weapons. They disdain the use of armor and shields. Only the lesser races need such protection.

Like all giant-kin, firbolg PCs seem strange and aloof to other player characters. Their motivations are different than those of smaller folk; for example, they often try to live up to the ideals of storm giants, making them seem even more strange to lesser folk.

Special Advantages. Firbolgs have magical powers usable once per day. These develop, in order, at odd-numbered levels, starting at 3rd level. The powers are: *detect magic, diminution* (as double the potion), *fools' gold, forget,* and *alter self.* These cannot be used when the firbolg is engaged in melee combat.

Firbolgs can use large human weapons (like two-handed swords and halberds) with one hand without penalty.

When using weapons of their own make (huge double-sized versions of human weapons), firbolg can wield them with both hands to inflict double damage.

Firbolgs can swat away incoming missiles with a roll of 6 or better on 1d20. With one free

hand, they can bat away up to two missiles per round. Large missiles, such as hurled boulders or catapult missiles, can be caught if the firbolg wishes. Caught missiles can be hurled back at opponents on the next round with a –2 penalty to the attack roll.

Special Disadvantages. Firbolgs have 15% magic resistance, even against magic that is beneficial.

Firbolgs never wear armor of any sort, nor do they carry shields.

Firbolgs take damage as large creatures.

When using man-made weapons, firbolg cannot apply their Strength bonuses.

Firbolgs must earn *double* the experience points of the base class to advance each level (for a fighter, 2nd level at 4,000, 3rd at 8,000, and so on).

Firbolg Shamans: Firbolg shamans must earn *triple* the experience points of the base clerical class to advance as shamans.

In addition, firbolg shamans gain additional innate magical abilities of the illusion/phantasm school. At 1st to 5th level, they receive two 1st level spells at each level. At 6th and 7th levels they receive two 2nd level spells. As innate abilities, these are randomly determined, and do not change once they are established. Each of these illusionist spells can be used once per day.

Monstrous Traits. Size.

Superstitions. Firbolg have an innate fear of human and demihuman mobs.

Weapon Proficiencies: Club, halberd, *giant-kin halberd, giant-kin two-handed sword*, two-handed sword.

Nonweapon Proficiencies: Agriculture, animal handling, animal training, blacksmithing, cooking, eating, gaming, herbalism, hunting, intimidation, reading/writing, set snares, weaponsmithing, weather sense.

Giant-kin, Voadkyn

Ability Score Adjustments. The initial ability scores are modified by a +1 bonus to Strength, a +2 bonus to Dexterity, a –1 penalty to Constitution, and a –2 penalty to Wisdom.

Ability Score Range

Ability	Minimum	Maximum
Strength	11	18
Dexterity	13	19
Constitution	8	16
Intelligence	11	17
Wisdom	3	16
Charisma	3	18

Class Restrictions

Class	Maximum Level
Warrior	
Fighter	11
Ranger	11
Paladin	—
Wizard	
Mage	8
Illusionist	—
Priest	
Cleric	—
Druid	—
Shaman	7
Witch Doctor	—
Rogue	
Thief	10
Bard	—

Hit Dice. Player character voadkyn receive hit dice by class. In addition, they receive 7 bonus hit points at first level.

Alignment. Voadkyn tend toward chaotic good. PC voadkyn may be of any alignment, but are usually chaotic good.

Natural Armor Class. 8.

Background. Voadkyn are also known by the more common name of wood giants. They are one of the smallest of the giant-kin races,

vaguely resembling giant-sized wood elves. They stand about 9½ feet tall and weigh approximately 700 pounds. They have the same physical proportions as humans, which gives them a thinner, lighter look than other giant-kin. Wood giants have no facial or body hair. They have large heads as compared to their bodies, and their jaws, chins and mouths are especially prominent. Their ears are on a higher plane than human ears, resting almost completely above the line of the eyes.

The skin of a wood giant can be any shade of brown mixed with yellow or green. They like to wear leather armor or ring mail, and they carry a special steel-tipped sheath for their sword which allows them to use it as a walking stick. They often disdain footwear, leaving their feet bare, though they do wrap their ankles in strips of leather. They dress in loose trousers or short kilts stained in forest colors, and always wear a leather forearm sheath to protect their bow arm.

Wood giants live in the same forests favored by wood elves, whom they are good friends with. In fact, the two races often co-exist. They share a bond that goes back further than the oldest legends. They do not make their own lairs, preferring to live under the stars or to share a wood elf lair when shelter is needed.

The bond between wood giants and wood elves extends to the other elven races. Wood giants tolerate the company of any good elves. Usually, they do not mix with other intelligent creatures, except for the occasional treant.

A small number of voadkyn have druid powers. Voadkyn druids are never found in the same community with voadkyn shamans.

Voadkyn are flighty and frivolous by nature. They have a fondness for finely cut gems and well-crafted magical items. They also love to eat and drink wine, usually in large amounts.

Languages. Voadkyn, treant, sylvan elf, common.

Role-Playing Suggestions. Wood giants give in to sudden whims and rarely take anything seriously. Those that decide to become adventurers are mostly in it for the fun they believe awaits them and for the treasures they believe they will earn. They are fun-loving beings. More serious companions consider them to be irrational, foolish, and even obnoxious. Still, most believe wood giants to be friendly and enjoyable company.

Voadkyn PCs are slightly more ambitious than those who remain in the forest, but they still appear to be unmotivated, plodding, even lazy beings. This temperament makes them slow to anger, but they will fight to defend themselves or their allies.

Wood giants love to eat, and they always have a sack of nuts and seeds from which to snack. When traveling with other adventurers, a wood giant can be heard munching on some plant byproduct almost constantly. They eat all kinds of vegetables and plants, including leaves and roots that other humanoid races find inedible. They do not eat meat.

Special Advantages. Wood giants, like elves, are 90% resistant to *sleep* and *charm* spells. They have infravision up to 90 feet.

At 7th level, wood giants gain the ability to

polymorph (self) into any humanoid creature, from three to 15 feet in height. They cannot form themselves into another specific person, only into a typical member of the race.

Voadkyn can move silently in forests, and any opponents there suffer a –4 penalty on their surprise rolls. In fact, voadkyn can blend into forest vegetation so well that only creatures able to detect invisible objects can see them. Voadkyn are quick, and can move out of hiding, fire an arrow, and return to their hiding place in the same round.

The favorite wood giant weapon, a huge long bow, gives a wood giant a +1 bonus to attack rolls and a 50% increase in range. The large-sized arrows for these bows cause 1d8 points of damage. The voadkyn must be at full size to use this bow.

Special Disadvantages. Voadkyn take damage as large creatures. They get no attack bonus for high strength.

Voadkyn warriors use the Paladin XP table.

Monstrous Traits. Size.

Superstitions. Voadkyn dislike enclosed spaces. They believe that nights when the stars are hidden precede days of ill fortune, and are reluctant to do much on such days.

Weapon Proficiencies: *Giant-kin dagger, giant-kin long bow, giant-kin mace,* two-handed sword.

Nonweapon Proficiencies: Alertness, animal lore, animal noise, animal training (dire wolves), bowyer/fletcher, direction sense, drinking, eating, fast-talking, gaming, hiding, hunting, set snares, survival (forests), wine-making.

Gnoll

Ability Score Adjustments. The initial ability scores are modified by a +1 bonus to Strength, and a –1 penalty to Intelligence and Charisma.

Ability Score Range

Ability	Minimum	Maximum
Strength	6	18
Dexterity	5	18
Constitution	5	18
Intelligence	3	14
Wisdom	3	16
Charisma	3	14

Class Restrictions

Class	Maximum Level
Warrior	
Fighter	11
Ranger	—
Paladin	—
Wizard	
Mage	—
Illusionist	—
Priest	
Cleric	9
Druid	—
Shaman	5
Witch Doctor	5
Rogue	
Thief	11
Bard	—

Hit Dice. Player character gnolls receive hit dice by class. In addition they receive 2 bonus hit points at first level.

Alignment. Gnolls tend toward chaotic evil. PC gnolls may be of any alignment, but are usually some form of neutral.

Natural Armor Class. 10.

Background. Gnolls are large, evil, hyena-like humanoids that roam the land in loosely organized bands. They stand about 7½ feet tall.

They are humanoid, but the fine details more closely resemble a hyena. The skin of a gnoll is greenish gray that gets darker near its muzzle. They have short manes of reddish gray to dull yellow hair.

Gnolls usually live beneath the ground or within abandoned ruins. Underground tribes operate mainly during the night. The strongest gnolls rule their brothers, using fear and intimidation to best advantage. Gnoll females fight as well as the males, though they rarely get to use the best armor and weapons available to the band.

Gnoll society uses slaves, and they often work with other humanoids, including orcs, bugbears, and trolls. This works best when the gnolls and their allies are of similar strength and numbers. If either gains an advantage, the other usually becomes food. To a gnoll, hunger comes before friendship or fear. They dislike goblins, kobolds, giants, humans, demi-humans, and any type of manual labor.

Languages. Gnoll, flind, troll, orc, hobgoblin, common.

Role-Playing Suggestions. Gnoll player characters are extremely rare, for it is very difficult for them to overcome their chaotic evil upbringing. Those who reject gnoll society usually do so out of hatred of the gnolls or to gain revenge against their race for some real or imagined wrong.

Those gnolls who become adventurers often exhibit evil tendencies. They fight a constant battle to keep their bestial urges in check, and to overcome their natural aversion to manual labor. They find it particularly hard to break their taste for intelligent creatures, as they are confirmed carnivores.

Gnoll adventurers will often put up with races they don't like out of necessity.

Special Advantages. None.

Special Disadvantages. Gnolls take damage as large creatures.

Monstrous Traits. Appearance, bestial habits.

Superstitions. Revere the phases of the moon, avoid bright light.

Weapon Proficiencies: Battle axe, long composite bow, morning star, two-handed sword, any pole arm.

Nonweapon Proficiencies: Animal training (hyenodon), close-quarter fighting, hiding, hunting, observation, tracking, wild fighting.

Gnoll, Flind

Ability Score Adjustments. The initial ability scores are modified by a +1 bonus to Strength and a –1 penalty to Charisma.

Ability Score Range

Ability	Minimum	Maximum
Strength	8	18
Dexterity	6	18
Constitution	6	18
Intelligence	3	16
Wisdom	3	16
Charisma	3	16

Class Restrictions

Class	Maximum Level
Warrior	
Fighter	12
Ranger	—
Paladin	—
Wizard	
Mage	—
Illusionist	—
Priest	
Cleric	9
Druid	—
Shaman	7
Witch Doctor	7
Rogue	
Thief	11
Bard	—

Hit Dice. Player character flinds receive hit dice by class.

Alignment. Flinds tend toward lawful evil. PC flinds may be of any alignment, but are usually lawful neutral.

Natural Armor Class. 10.

Background. Flinds appear similar to gnolls, though they are shorter and broader. The average flind stands 6½ feet tall. They are more muscular than regular gnolls, and usually stronger. Short brown and red fur covers their bodies, and their ears are more rounded than the gnolls.

Flinds are looked upon with awe by gnolls, revered as leaders and heroes by the hyena-like humanoids. Otherwise, they have the same lifestyle as gnolls, except that they are not as chaotic. Flinds tend to get along with orcs, hobgoblins, bugbears, and ogres, but dislike and will not cooperate with trolls.

Languages. Flind, gnoll, orc, hobgoblin, bugbear, ogre, common.

Role-Playing Suggestions. If any type of gnoll is likely to become a player character, it is the flind. As they are already looked upon as heroes by their gnoll cousins, some flinds reject their evil natures to become heroes in the larger world. A rare few even become lawful good.

Flind PCs believe themselves to be very special. All of the reverence heaped upon them by the gnolls throughout their lives gives them a sense of worth not displayed often in humanoid cultures. They exhibit the same bestial urges as their gnoll cousins, but they can control them with less difficulty.

Special Advantages. A flind can use a *flindbar* to disarm an opponent. A hit requires an opponent to save vs. wands. A failed save means the weapon is entangled and ripped from the opponent's grasp.

Special Disadvantages. None

Monstrous Traits. Appearance, bestial habits.

Superstitions. Like gnolls, flinds hold a special reverence for the moon and its phases.

Weapon Proficiencies: Club, *flindbar*, glaive, long bow, long sword.

Nonweapon Proficiencies: Animal lore, close-quarter fighting, danger sense, direction sense, endurance, fortune telling, local history, looting, hunting, intimidation, reading/writing, religion, spellcraft, weaponsmithing.

Goblin

Ability Score Adjustments. The initial ability scores are modified by a −1 penalty to Strength and Charisma.

Ability Score Range

Ability	Minimum	Maximum
Strength	4	15
Dexterity	4	17
Constitution	5	16
Intelligence	3	18
Wisdom	3	18
Charisma	3	12

Class Restrictions

Class	Maximum Level
Warrior	
Fighter	10
Ranger	—
Paladin	—
Wizard	
Mage	—
Illusionist	—
Priest	
Cleric	9
Druid	—
Shaman	7
Witch Doctor	7
Rogue	
Thief	12
Bard —	

Hit Dice. Player character goblins receive hit dice by class.

Alignment. Goblins tend toward lawful evil. PC goblins may be of any alignment, but are usually lawful neutral.

Natural Armor Class. 10.

Background. Goblins are small humanoids, growing to a height of about four feet tall. They have flat faces, broad noses, pointed ears, wide mouths, and small, sharp fangs. Though they walk upright, their arms hang down to their knees. Their dull, glazed eyes range in color from bright red to gleaming yellow. Their speech is harsh and of a higher pitch than humans.

These humanoids are generally evil in nature, and often they are great cowards as well. They avoid direct confrontations whenever possible, preferring the safety of ambushes. They use simple, even crude, strategies and tactics. They do not believe in fair fights, for many-on-one works much better than one-on-one to the goblin mindset.

Goblins live in dank caves and dismal underground dwellings. They only come above ground at night or on dark, cloudy days. Goblins and their lairs carry a foul stench, due to their lack of sanitation. Their tribes share with large common areas set aside for eating and sleeping. Treasure and property belongs to the entire tribe, though the chief and his subchiefs watch over it. Only their leaders have separate living areas.

Females are not afforded the same rights as males in goblin society, and females never learn to fight. Their role is to service the males and care for the young.

Each tribe has an exact pecking order, and every goblin knows his exact place in it. The way to move up the social ladder is through battle, and goblins constantly fight among themselves to improve their station in life.

Tribes regularly take slaves for food and labor. They keep their slaves constantly shackled and under guard.

Goblins take great pleasure in killing. They do not eat much, but they eat almost anything. Rats, snakes, humans, and other humanoids make up the bulk of their diets. When food is scarce, they will even eat carrion. They hate most other humanoid races, especially gnomes and dwarves.

Languages. Goblin, kobold, orc, hobgoblin, common.

Role-Playing Suggestions. Like most evil creatures, few goblins ever become adventurers. Those that do are unusually rare, for the individualistic life of an adventurer is completely foreign to goblin society. Those few members of the race who display such tendencies are often killed by their brethren, for they are believed to be insane.

If they can survive the prejudices and fears of their own people, goblin PCs generally reject their own societies. They leave their lairs and strike out to find fame (of a sort) and fortune (whatever they can get their hands on). They often fight against such goblin practices as slave keeping and marauding, working to make up for the atrocities of their people.

Still, you can't take all of the monster out of goblin PCs. They do their best to control their fear and overcome their natural cowardice, but few goblin PCs will earn awards for bravery. Even the cleanest goblin adventurers have trouble eliminating the stench they have grown up with. It hangs about them like a shroud. Because of their communal back-grounds, goblins have no concept of

privacy. This can lead to amusing — and not so amusing — situations for goblin PCs and their companions.

Special Advantages. Goblins have infravision to 60 feet. They can detect new or unusual construction in an underground area 25% of the time (1 or 2 on 1d8).

Goblin shamans can reach 7th level and have access to the spheres of divination, healing (reversed), protection, and sun (reversed).

Special Disadvantages. Bright light hurts goblin eyes, giving them a –1 penalty to their attack rolls when in bright sunshine.

Monstrous Traits. Appearance, bestial habits.

Superstitions. Eternal hatred and fear of gnomes and dwarves, sensitive to unusual behavior of worgs and wolves, fearful of dreams and visions.

Weapon Proficiencies: Axe, military pick, morning star, sling, short sword, spear.

Nonweapon Proficiencies: Alertness, animal handling, animal training (worg), begging, chanting, close-quarter fighting, fast-talking, fortune telling, hiding, hunting, information gathering, looting, mining, religion, riding (worg), set snares.

Hobgoblin

Ability Score Adjustments. The initial ability scores are modified by a –1 penalty to Charisma.

Ability Score Range

Ability	Minimum	Maximum
Strength	6	18
Dexterity	6	18
Constitution	5	18
Intelligence	3	18
Wisdom	3	18
Charisma	3	14

Class Restrictions

Class	Maximum Level
Warrior	
Fighter	11
Ranger	—
Paladin	—
Wizard	
Mage	—
Illusionist	—
Priest	
Cleric	9
Druid	—
Shaman	7
Witch Doctor	7
Rogue	
Thief	12
Bard	—

Hit Dice. Player character hobgoblins receive hit dice by class.

Alignment. Hobgoblins tend toward lawful evil. PC hobgoblins may be of any alignment, though they are usually lawful neutral.

Natural Armor Class. 10.

Background. Hobgoblins are stocky humanoids with hairy, dark red to dark gray hides. The typical hobgoblin is 6½ feet tall, has yellow or dark brown eyes, and sharp yellow teeth. They favor brightly colored garments, especially outfits of blood red.

This fierce race wages a perpetual war against other humanoid races. They exist in a military society, proud of their status, their fighting prowess, their battle standards, and the quality of their weapons. War is their way of life, and to be a warrior is the highest calling a hobgoblin can have. Even when different tribes of hobgoblins meet, there will likely be verbal abuse (85%) or open warfare (15%) unless a strong leader is present.

Most hobgoblins dwell in subterranean complexes. A few tribes build fortified surface villages (about 20%). Hobgoblins consider themselves superior to the "lesser races," lording over goblins and orcs whenever possible.

The lesser races have only one good purpose to the hobgoblin mindset — they make decent battle fodder. In mixed groups, hobgoblins often serve as officers in units of goblins or orcs.

Hobgoblins have an extreme hatred of elves. When their opponents consist of mixed races, they always seek to destroy elves first.

Languages. Hobgoblin, orc, goblin, common, carnivorous ape (rare).

Role-Playing Suggestions. To hobgoblins, war is almost a religious experience. They fight for the glory of battle and to cause carnage, not to expand territory or right wrongs against them. Their outlook on war is much more pure than that. Conflict and strife are their meat and drink.

Hobgoblin PCs are rare in the extreme, but those that do take up the life of adventurers usually fall into one of two patterns. The first is the hobgoblin pacifist. These individuals detest war, though they may be extremely good at its brutal arts. Having grown tired of the constant fighting, they leave their tribes and seek to find a new life somewhere away from their people. Of course, as battle is what

they do best, they often find themselves using their militaristic arts to earn a living. However, at least as an adventurer they only have to fight when absolutely necessary. These type of characters will often wait until the last minute before entering a fray — not because they are cowards, but because they grow sick and tired of shedding blood.

The second pattern of hobgoblin PCs are those who turn away from the evil of their society. They reject the hobgoblin gods and perhaps even discover the faith of a non-evil deity. These characters seek to make amends for their old life styles, trying to repair the damage the hobgoblins have done and continue to do in the name of glorious war.

Even the best hobgoblin PCs find it hard to overcome all of their natural tendencies. Brutality, stoicism, courage, and cold-bloodedness are always with them, like dark cloaks they can never shed.

Special Advantages. Hobgoblins have infravision with a range of 60 feet.

They can detect new construction, sloping passages, and shifting walls in underground complexes 40% of the time (1-4 on 1d10).

Special Disadvantages. Most other humanoid and human societies attack hobgoblins on sight. Dwarves receive a +1 bonus to attack rolls against hobgoblins due to racial hatred.

Monstrous Traits. Appearance.

Superstitions. Weakness is feared and actively destroyed in hobgoblin society. A weapon which breaks during combat is an extremely bad omen.

Weapon Proficiencies: Long composite bow, morning star, scimitar, spear, whip, any pole arm.

Nonweapon Proficiencies: Armorer, blacksmithing, bowyer/fletcher, brewing, chanting, close-quarter fighting, direction sense, fire-building, hiding, intimidation, looting, religion, weaponsmithing, wild fighting.

Kobold

Ability Score Adjustments. The initial ability scores are modified by a –1 penalty to Strength and Constitution.

Ability Score Range

Ability	Minimum	Maximum
Strength	3	16
Dexterity	4	18
Constitution	4	15
Intelligence	3	17
Wisdom	3	18
Charisma	3	14

Class Restrictions

Class	Maximum Level
Warrior	
Fighter	8
Ranger	—
Paladin	—
Wizard	
Mage	—
Illusionist	—
Priest	
Cleric	9
Druid	—
Shaman	7
Witch Doctor	7
Rogue	
Thief	12
Bard	—

Hit Dice. Player character kobolds receive hit dice by class.

Alignment. Kobolds tend toward lawful evil. PC kobolds may be of any alignment, though they are usually lawful neutral.

Natural Armor Class. 10.

Background. Kobolds are short humanoids, growing to a height of three feet. They have scaly hides of dark brown to rusty black, and smell awful to anything but another kobold. The eyes of a kobold glow bright red, and they

have two small horns atop their dog-like heads.

Kobolds are masters of trickery, but they prefer tactics where they can apply overwhelming odds. They have a racial hatred of gnomes and are willing to attack these demihumans on sight. The only way they will go against humans and other demihumans is if they have superior numbers — at least two to one, more if they can manage it. They have learned to use swarming attacks, throwing themselves at opponents in large waves.

Most kobolds are a sadistic, cowardly lot. Their lairs and ambush sites are studded with concealed pit traps. They line the bottom of these pits with additional hazards, such as spikes or water traps, hoping to catch and incapacitate larger creatures with them.

Kobolds set up lairs in dark, damp underground locations and deep in overgrown forests. They are good miners, often settling in areas that show mining promise. These humanoids set out from their territories to forage for plants, hunt for meat, and to waylay humans and demihumans. They capture victims to use as food or to sell into slavery (if there is a market for such wares in the vicin-

ity). Strangers are not trusted, and they have a particular hatred of brownies, pixies, sprites, and gnomes. Gnomes, especially, are shown no quarter, and kobolds will never eat them.

The conquest of land is the ultimate goal of all kobold tribes. They rejoice in stripping a land of its resources, and they love to accumulate power. As they have a deep hatred of all other life, they find great delight in killing.

Languages. Kobold, orc, goblin, common.

Role-Playing Suggestions. Kobolds strive to be taken seriously by the larger races. They hate jokes directed at their diminutive size and strength, and seek to make up for their shortcomings through ferocity and tenacity. To other races, their language sounds like the yapping of small dogs, and few can take them seriously unless they are in large numbers.

Kobold PCs break the model of typical specimens of the race. There are those who reject the racial hatreds and savage practices of their fellows. Others discover the faith of a kinder god, and seek to learn and spread such faith to others. A few have no stomach for fighting and bloodshed, and these become rogues who go adventuring to escape the life they were born into.

Whatever the case, kobold PCs have a harder edge than other character types. They retain their dislike of short jokes, and they are often belligerent, wise-cracking, and pushy, as they must make up for their small size in whatever way they can. Even the most pleasant of the race are a little mean-spirited.

Kobolds, especially kobold rogues, like to keep in practice with their skills of trickery, ambushing, and setting traps. Some few take to inventing, applying their cleverness and ingenuity to non-fatal mechanisms.

Special Advantages. Kobolds can see in the dark, up to 60 feet with their infravision. Unless kobold characters display special capabilities, intelligent and powerful opponents are likely to attack them last of all.

Special Disadvantages. Bright light hinders

kobolds, making it difficult for them to see. When forced to fight in sunlit conditions or the equivalent, kobolds receive a –1 penalty to their attack rolls. Gnomes have a +1 bonus when attacking kobolds.

Monstrous Traits. Appearance, dog-like voices, bestial habits.

Superstitions. Fear of spellcasters, fear and hatred of larger races, hatred of gnomes.

Weapon Proficiencies: Club (spiked), hand axe, javelin, short sword, spear.

Nonweapon Proficiencies: Animal noise, animal training (giant weasel), animal training (wild boar), begging, close-quarter fighting, danger sense, fast-talking, gem cutting, hiding, looting, mining, set snares, wild fighting.

Lizard Man

Ability Score Adjustments. There are no adjustments to the basic ability scores.

Ability Score Range

Ability	Minimum	Maximum
Strength	8	18
Dexterity	3	18
Constitution	6	18
Intelligence	3	17
Wisdom	3	18
Charisma	3	16

Class Restrictions

Class	Maximum Level
Warrior	
Fighter	12
Ranger	—
Paladin	—
Wizard	
Mage	—
Illusionist	—
Priest	
Cleric	—
Druid	—
Shaman	7
Witch Doctor	—
Rogue	
Thief	9
Bard	—

Hit Dice. Player character lizard men receive hit dice by class.

Alignment. Lizard men tend toward true neutral alignment. PC lizard men may be of any alignment.

Natural Armor Class. 5.

Background. Lizard men are the natural rulers of the swamps they inhabit. These savage, semi-aquatic, reptilian humanoids live through scavenging and raiding. The less hostile tribes tend to be fishers and gatherers, though there seem to be more of the violent, war-loving tribes scattered across the land.

Lizard men grow to heights between six and seven feet tall. The average weight of these humanoids is between 200 and 250 pounds. Their coloration ranges from dark green to gray to brown, and scales cover most of their bodies. Lizard men have three- to four-foot-long tails, which are not prehensile. Only those very familiar with the race can tell the difference between males and females. They wear only the simplest of ornamentation — strings of bone and other barbaric items.

Lizard men usually dwell in marshes and swamps. They live underwater in air-filled caves, emerging to hunt, forage, and raid nearby communities — including other lizard man camps. Most tribes have about 150 members, including females and hatchlings. The tribes sometimes form loose alliances against common enemies, though these last only as long as the threat is obvious.

These omnivorous humanoids eat almost anything. The foulest, most savage tribes crave human flesh. Tales of these savage lizard men ambushing humans abound, for they seek both living and dead flesh to feast upon.

A small number of lizard man tribes have

evolved to a higher level of civilization, and it is from these tribes that PC lizard men are assumed to come. These lizard men live in crude huts, make and use shields, and have discovered the benefits of ranged weapons. They make and use barbed darts and javelins, use crude clubs in melee, and some have learned to capture and use the weapons of humans and demihumans.

Languages. Lizard man, common.

Role-Playing Suggestions. Lizard men are barbarians. Even those from the advanced tribes are considered savages by the civilized world. When a lizard man PC enters a campaign, he faces many of the same problems which confront barbaric humans — the ways he knows are not the ways of culture and civilization. The lizard man character has left the swamps behind, but his savage nature remains. Perhaps, as a member of an advanced tribe, he has decided to learn more of the wonders of the civilized world. Once he has amassed enough knowledge, he will return to his tribe to teach them. Or, as a member of a more primitive tribe, the character has been forcefully taken from the swamps and thrust into the outer world. Now he fights beside adventurers until he can find his way home — or just because he likes the violence in which his new companions get involved.

Lizard men are known for their strength, their natural cunning, and their alien ways. They should be played as true outsiders — not only are they from different lands and primitive cultures, but they are reptilian. Lizard men have a much different outlook on the world than mammals. They are born from eggs, they spend much of their life in water, and they are closer to the natural laws of survival than their civilized counterparts. They should be played as alien minds, with alien tastes, and alien perceptions. Often, a lizard man will be at odds with his companions as to the way to proceed. "Eat-or-die" is often the basic instinct running through a lizard man's mind, and this does not

always go along with adventurers' ideals of honor, chivalry, and fairness.

As a savage, the lizard man PC is in tune with the natural world. This does not mean he is an avid protector of nature (as centaurs, for example, are wont to be), but that he understands nature's signs and can survive in places others would find inhospitable. Remember also, lizard men PCs do not understand civilization very well. They will often be alarmed, frightened, or offended by many of its most common features.

In combat, lizard man warriors fight as individuals. The civilized concepts of cooperation and strict planning are unknown to him, and he will often find his own course in any battle. Against equal or lesser opponents, a lizard man may charge directly into the fray. When facing superior opponents, a lizard man may turn to wily tactics or sheer ferocity. The savage warrior has a few weaknesses, however. He can be distracted by food and simple treasures, even in the midst of battle.

Special Advantages. Lizard men can move in water at a rate of 12. They have no move-ment or attack penalties when in water, and receive swimming as a bonus proficiency.

Lizard men can remain under water for long periods of time before they need to draw air. In game terms, a lizard man can hold his breath up to 2/3 his Constitution score in rounds (rounded up).

Special Disadvantages. Lizard men are fairly slow and clumsy on land, having a base move-ment rate of 6.

Lizard men must wet their entire bodies once a day. If they are unable to find adequate amounts of moisture (a full waterskin is enough), they begin to lose Constitution at a rate of 3 points per day. If their Constitution falls to zero, they die from dehydration.

If food (which could include a fallen friend or foe) or treasure appear during a battle, a lizard man must make a successful Wisdom check to keep his mind on the battle. Failure means he turns away from the fight to feast or gather spoils. This distraction lasts at least one round. Every additional round, the lizard man can attempt to break away from the distraction by making another Wisdom check.

Lizard man warriors start with two weapon proficiencies. Other classes start with one.

Lizard men with a SPELLJAMMER® origin cannot be multi-classed; however, these start with the normal number of proficiencies and access to more advanced weaponry and armor (armor costs are double standard prices).

Monstrous Traits. Monstrous appearance, bestial fear, bestial habits.

Superstitions. Lizard men fear dry heat and locations with dry heat, such as deserts.

Weapon Proficiencies: Battle axe (stone), *great club* (morning star), barbed dart, javelin.

Nonweapon Proficiencies: Alertness, danger sense, direction sense, fishing, herbalism, hiding, hunting, natural fighting, survival (swamps).

Minotaur

Ability Score Adjustments. The initial ability scores are modified by a +2 bonus to Strength and Constitution, and a –2 penalty to Wisdom and Charisma.

Ability Score Range

Ability	Minimum	Maximum
Strength	12	20
Dexterity	5	14
Constitution	12	20
Intelligence	5	14
Wisdom	3	16
Charisma	3	16

Class Restrictions

Class	Maximum Level
Warrior	
Fighter	12
Ranger	8
Paladin	—
Wizard	
Mage	8
Illusionist	—
Priest	
Cleric	—
Druid	—
Shaman	—
Witch Doctor	7
Rogue	
Thief	10
Bard	—

Hit Dice. Player character minotaurs receive hit dice by class. In addition, they receive 6 bonus hit points at first level.

Alignment. Minotaurs tend toward chaotic evil. PC minotaurs may be of any alignment.

Natural Armor Class. 6.

Background. These details are for general play in the standard campaign worlds. Minotaurs elsewhere may differ (notably those of Krynn, the DRAGONLANCE® setting).

Most minotaurs are either cursed humans or the offspring of minotaurs and humans. All of these minotaurs are male, very muscular and broad, and very tall (7 to 7½ feet tall). They have the head of a bull and the body of a human male. They usually live in a very primitive fashion, in caves, forests, or ruins.

Minotaurs venerate physical strength above all else. The strong, they believe, should naturally rule. Surrender is viewed as weakness, so minotaurs fight (or argue) to the death. They are extremely cunning and have excellent senses. They will attack without fear and retreat only if the opponent is obviously beyond their ability to defeat.

While many minotaurs are brutal, uncivilized savages, they are not mindless killers. Most are ruthless, harsh, and stubborn, but some are thoughtful and even sophisticated. A few are known for gentleness and kindness.

Languages. Minotaur, common.

Role-Playing Suggestions. Much of the impetus for role-playing a minotaur can involve reclaiming a lost human heritage, or finding some way to fit into the campaign world in a civilized manner.

Though the curse that afflicts some minotaurs makes them chaotic, adventuring minotaurs usually reject the evil that others of their kind embrace. However, they value strength, and may be seduced by the idea that might makes right. Also, any opportunity to alleviate their curse is grabbed for, perhaps to the exclusion of reason and safety.

In general, however, they make valuable, if unpredictable, allies.

Special Advantages. Minotaurs receive a +2 bonus to their surprise rolls. They can track prey by scent 50% of the time. They are immune to *maze* spells and receive a +3 bonus to their morale scores (including saves vs. magical fear). They have 60' infravision.

Special Disadvantages. Minotaurs take damage as large creatures.

Monstrous Traits. Appearance, bestial habits.

Superstitions. They dislike spell casters.

Weapon Proficiencies: Flail, great axe (same characteristics as halberd), oaken club.

Nonweapon Proficiencies: Alertness, animal noise, blind-fighting, direction sense, drinking, eating, hunting, intimidation, natural fighting, religion, seamanship, tracking, wild fighting.

Mongrelman

Ability Score Adjustments. The initial ability scores are modified by a –1 penalty to Intelligence and Charisma. The player can add a +1 bonus to any other ability score, not to exceed the starting maximum.

Ability Score Range

Ability	Minimum	Maximum
Strength	6	17
Dexterity	6	18
Constitution	8	18
Intelligence	3	17
Wisdom	3	18
Charisma	2	8

Class Restrictions

Class	Maximum Level
Warrior	
Fighter	10
Ranger	—
Paladin	—
Wizard	
Mage	10
Illusionist	—
Priest	
Cleric	10
Druid	—
Shaman	7
Witch Doctor	—
Rogue	
Thief	12
Bard	8*

* Can adjust crowd reactions only among own kind. Other crowds will react negatively.

Hit Dice. Player character mongrelmen receive hit dice by class.

Alignment. Mongrelmen tend toward lawful neutral. Player character mongrelmen may be of any alignment.

Natural Armor Class. 5.

Background. Mongrelmen combine the worst features of many species, including humans, orcs, gnolls, ogres, dwarves, hobgoblins, elves, bugbears, and bullywugs. No two mongrelmen look the same, but all appear as poorly constructed combinations of various humanoid races.

Always misshapen and ugly, mongrelmen grow to heights ranging from five to seven feet tall. In general, they are ashamed of their appearance and do their best to keep their bodies hidden from those they encounter. Mongrelmen speak common, though they intermix intelligible words with grunts, whistles, growls, and gestures. Their names often mimic animal noises.

Mongrelmen receive no welcome in lawful and good societies. Among evil and chaotic groups, they meet with enslavement and abuse. Most of these reactions are in response to mongrelmen appearances — they look like deformed monsters and are treated as such by society at large.

They work as slaves or serfs, toiling endlessly for cruel and evil masters. Mongrelmen have infinite patience and an unswerving belief that their oppressors will eventually be punished by outside forces. Because of this belief, enslaved mongrelmen refuse to rebel against their masters, even when the opportunity presents itself. Those remaining free often take up residence in abandoned ruins or other long-forgotten places.

Mongrelmen are survivors. To remain alive and relatively unharmed is their ultimate goal — they do not seek power or treasure or fame like other races. An orderly day-to-day existence is a mongrelman's perfect state of being. Patience is the greatest virtue, not the ability to destroy. They are by no means pacifists, but they will only fight in self-defense or on the orders of their masters.

Free mongrelmen have a long tradition of art, music, and literature. Of course, mongrelman music is an acquired taste, being a bizarre cacophony of animal songs mixed with mournful dirges and wails.

Languages. Common.

Role-Playing Suggestions. Mongrelmen player characters are either escaped slaves whose masters finally succumbed to outside forces (as the mongrelman knew they would) or free mongrelmen who have been inspired by some ballad or tale to take up the life of an adventurer. While fighting is not in their blood, mongrelmen make natural thieves and a few aspire to become bards or even wizards.

Even the most outgoing mongrelman is shy, quiet, and easily embarrassed. The shame that makes them conceal their bodies follows even the most successful adventurer throughout his or her career. They hate what they look like, and sometimes turn to adventuring in order to

forget for a time. Of course, most people they meet are quick to remind them with a gasp, by turning away, or by outright insults.

When speaking in character, players should punctuate their sentences with grunts, whistles, and animal noises. Lots of gestures are also used by mongrelmen when they talk. Those mongrelmen PCs who believe themselves to be artistically inclined should also feel free to make up ballads, stories, and songs on the spot to entertain their companions — the more awful and abstract the song, the more perfect it will be to a mongrelman's ears.

Mongrelmen are great believers in what will be will be. This makes them infinitely patient and extremely ordered. Those that become adventurers may have decided that fate needs a little help now and then, but they still hold to the belief that everything is planned and they can't change it. Of course, most feel that something good is waiting for them in the future. All they have to do is wait patiently for it to arrive.

Shyness is bred into mongrelmen, and even those of the race that work as adventurers tend to stay out of the spotlight. They like to avoid contact with others (except their companions), and have come to believe that stealing what they need (but never more than they need) is perfectly acceptable.

They love art, music, and literature. Most read everything they can get their hands on. Often, when their party discovers scrolls or books, mongrelmen PCs will try to acquire them instead of seeking magical weapons, items, or even gold.

Special Advantages. Mongrelmen can *mimic* the sounds made by any monster or creature they have encountered, though they cannot imitate special attack forms.

All mongrelmen, regardless of class, can *pick pockets*. They have a base score of 70%, and receive a 5% bonus in pickpocket per level, starting at 5th level.

Mongrelmen can *camouflage* themselves and their items. It takes one full turn to hide, giving them an 80% base chance to go unnoticed. Each additional turn spent preparing the camouflage increases the chance by 1% to a maximum of 95% (after 16 turns). Successfully camouflaged stationary persons and items are not noticed unless they are touched or otherwise disturbed. Camouflaged buildings are usually unnoticeable farther away than 50 feet, though this depends on the size and type of the structure.

Special Disadvantages. No matter what Charisma score a mongrelman has among his own kind, when first meeting strangers of different races his Charisma is treated as 1 for reaction adjustments.

Monstrous Traits. Appearance, using animal noises when they speak.

Superstitions. Mongrelmen believe strongly in predestination, fear other humanoids (who hunt them for sport), and fear manifestations of the supernatural,

Weapon Proficiencies: Broad sword, club, long sword, short sword, morning star, quarterstaff, blowgun (rare).

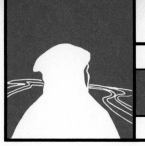

Nonweapon Proficiencies: Acting, agriculture, animal handling, animal noise, artistic ability, begging, brewing, chanting, craft instrument, dancing, disguise, etiquette, fortune telling, herbalism, hiding, information gathering, observation, poetry, reading/writing, religion, spellcraft, ventriloquism, voice mimicry.

Ogre, Half-Ogre

Ability Score Adjustments. The initial ability scores are modified as follows:
- *Ogre:* +2 Str, +2 Con; –2 Int, –2 Cha
- *Half-Ogre:* +1 Str, +1 Con; –1 Int, –1 Cha

Ability Score Range (Ogre/Half-Ogre)

Ability	Minimum	Maximum
Strength	16/14	20/18
Dexterity	2/3	8/12
Constitution	14/14	20/19
Intelligence	2/3	8/12
Wisdom	2/2	9/12
Charisma	2/2	8/8

Class Restrictions (Ogre/Half-Ogre)

Class	Maximum Level
Warrior	
Fighter	12/12
Ranger	—/—
Paladin	—/—
Wizard	
Mage	—/—
Illusionist	—/—
Priest	
Cleric	—/4
Druid	—/—
Shaman	3/4
Witch Doctor	—/4
Rogue	
Thief	—/—
Bard	—/—

Hit Dice. Player character ogres and half-ogres receive hit dice by class. In addition, they receive 4 bonus hit points at first level.

Alignment. Ogres tend toward chaotic evil Half-ogres tend toward chaotic neutral. PC ogres and half-ogres may be of any alignment.

Natural Armor Class. Ogres have a natural armor class of 5. Half-ogres have a natural armor class of 8.

Background. Ogres are big, ugly humanoids that stand over nine feet tall. Most are greedy, living by ambushing, raiding, and outright theft. They tend to be ill-tempered beings, nasty and very violent. Dark warty bumps cover their dead yellow hides. They have purple and white eyes, orange or black teeth and talons, and long, greasy hair that ranges in color from blackish-blue to dark green.

Ogres live by raiding and scavenging. They will eat anything. In the wild, they have a fondness for elf, dwarf, and halfling flesh. They use prisoners as slaves or save them for food. They have ravenous natures — they covet everything they see. As such, they can rarely be trusted, and they squabble over treasure even among their own kind.

Most ogres are a plague upon humanity. They constantly seek gold, gems, jewelry, and human and demihuman flesh. Few develop crafts of their own, and even fewer perform any form of productive labor for themselves.

Half-ogres: These are the offspring of ogre and human matings. They have much of the strength and size of their ogre heritage, but also retain much of the native intelligence and reason of their human side. Half-ogres stand between seven and eight feet tall, appearing as huge humans. The skin coloration that marks ogres is very much subdued in half-ogres: swarthy skin, lank hair and usually, but not always, human eyes.

Languages. Ogre, orc, troll, stone giant, gnoll, common. Half-ogre player characters will nearly always have common as their native language.

their unusual size, they look much like ugly humans. This makes it easier for them to find a place in human society, even if they must hide part of their heritage. Half-ogre PCs should select a monstrous trait which emerges under certain circumstances in order to give them the feel of playing a humanoid character.

Special Advantages. Shamans (both types) have access to the spheres of combat, divination, healing, protection, and sun (PCs are not required to reverse sun spells if they are of good or neutral alignment).

Special Disadvantages. Ogres and half ogres take damage as large creatures. They have attack roll penalties when fighting gnomes and dwarves. Ogres are –4 against both, half-ogres are –4 against gnomes and –2 against dwarves.

Monstrous Traits. Size, appearance, bestial habits.

Superstitions. Fear of sickness, fear of physical weakness, fear of the god known as the Destroyer.

Weapon Proficiencies: Club, *goblin stick*, halberd, spear, two-handed sword, voulge.

Nonweapon Proficiencies: Drinking, eating, fire-building, hunting, intimidation, religion, tracking, wild fighting.

Ogre Mage

Ability Score Adjustments. The initial ability scores are modified by a +1 bonus to Strength, and a –2 penalty to Wisdom.

Ability Score Range

Ability	Minimum	Maximum
Strength	12	18
Dexterity	7	18
Constitution	8	14
Intelligence	8	17
Wisdom	3	16
Charisma	2	14

Role-Playing Suggestions. The ogre that becomes an adventurer is very, very rare. It is very difficult for ogres to overcome their chaotic evil natures and their love for human and demihuman flesh. Those that do have rejected ogre society and morals, becoming outcasts in their own communities. They have turned away from their evil sides, though they often retain their chaotic natures.

Many ogre PCs are kind and gentle — at least by ogre standards. They befriend or are befriended by adventurers (see Chapter One), and decide to join the "tribe" of their new friends. As part of the adventuring tribe, ogre PCs will do their best to fit in and act like their companions, though mistakes and slip ups are bound to occur. They especially have a hard time containing their avaricious tendencies, wanting every piece of treasure the group stumbles upon.

Half-Ogres: Half-ogres have an easier time of it, for their monstrous sides are tempered by human thoughts and emotions. Except for

Class Restrictions

Class	Maximum Level
Warrior	
Fighter	9
Ranger	—
Paladin	—
Wizard	
Mage	8
Illusionist	—
Priest	
Cleric	—
Druid	—
Shaman	7
Witch Doctor	—
Rogue	
Thief	8
Bard	—

Hit Dice. Player character ogre magi receive hit dice by class. In addition they receive 5 bonus hit points at first level.

Alignment. Ogre magi tend toward lawful evil. PC ogre magi may be of any lawful alignment.

Natural Armor Class. 4.

Background. Ogre magi have light blue, light green, or pale brown skin. Ivory horns jut from their foreheads. They are 10½ feet tall, with black nails, dark eyes with white pupils, and white teeth and tusks. They favor oriental clothing, armor, and weapons.

These larger, more intelligent ogre magi live in fortified dwellings or caves. They raid for slaves, treasure and food, and are very protective of their young. They follow many oriental traditions, including respect and honor for their clans and clan symbols.

Ogre magi are more civilized than their primitive, smaller cousins. This does not make them less fierce or dangerous, just smarter and more cultured. They prefer to use magic instead of physical force, and are much more reflective than normal ogres.

Ogre magi shamans are usually female.

Languages. Ogre magi, ogre, common.

Role-Playing Suggestions. Ogre magi that become player characters often do so because of a particular need, or because they are forced into it. Those who strike out for a particular need are often driven by the desire to learn (usually magic) or to find some special item that their clan requires. These individuals will work with adventurers for as long as it benefits their personal goals. An ogre mage may become a forced outcast for some crime against the clan (be it real or imagined). The ogre mage must find a way to regain honor and status, but until then will take up the life of an adventurer. Others are cast out because they fail to display the proper attitudes of the ogre magi. These individuals might follow good or neutral alignments, or seek to change long-standing traditions.

A few ogre magi are kidnapped when they are very young and raised away from their clans. These PCs have little knowledge about their heritage, but display tendencies which match the people who raised them. In the case of those kept as slaves, their adventuring days usually begin when they gain their freedom. While they might be interested in finding their

clans, these ogre magi usually find themselves alone and without any culture or society to call their own.

Special Advantages. Ogre magi develop special abilities as they gain hit dice: 1) assume *gaseous form* once per day (as the potion), *fly* for 12 turns; 2) become *invisible* at will, *charm person* once per day; 3) cast *sleep* once per day, *regenerate* one hit point per round (lost members must be reattached to regenerate); 4) *cause darkness* in a 10-foot radius at will; 5) *polymorph* to a human or similar biped creature (4 feet to 12 feet in height), *cone of cold* once per day (creates a 60-foot cone, 20 feet in diameter at the far end, that inflicts 8d8 points of damage, save vs. spells for half damage).

Ogre magi are +1 on morale.

Special Disadvantages. Ogre magi take damage as large creatures. Oriental equipment is often both rare and expensive.

Ogre magi must earn twice as many XP as a human character to advance each level (2nd level fighter at 4,000 XP, 3rd at 8,000, etc).

Monstrous Traits. Size, appearance.

Superstitions. Ogre magi fear losing honor or disgracing their clans. Optionally, the character can use the Honor system from the *Oriental Adventures* book.

Weapon Proficiencies: *Daikyu, katana, naginata,* scimitar, *tetsubo, wakizashi,* whip; oriental versions of the halberd, spear, and trident.

Nonweapon Proficiencies: Acting, armorer, bowyer/fletcher, etiquette, fortune telling, poetry, reading/writing, spellcraft, weaponsmithing, weaving, wild fighting.

Orc, Half-Orc

Ability Score Adjustments. The initial ability scores are modified as follows:
- *Orc:* +1 Str; –2 Cha
- *Half-Orc:* +1 Str, +1 Con; –2 Cha

Ability Score Range (Orc/Half-Orc)

Ability	Minimum	Maximum
Strength	6/6	18/18
Dexterity	3/3	17/17
Constitution	8/13	18/19
Intelligence	3/3	16/17
Wisdom	3/3	16/14
Charisma	3/3	12/12

Class Restrictions (Orc/Half-Orc)

Class	Maximum Level
Warrior	
Fighter	10/10*
Ranger	—/—
Paladin	—/—
Wizard	
Mage	—/—
Illusionist	—/—
Priest	
Cleric	9/4*
Druid	—/—
Shaman	6/4*
Witch Doctor	6/4*
Rogue	
Thief	11/8*
Bard	—/—

* Single-classed characters can rise higher

Hit Dice. Player character orcs and half-orcs receive hit dice by class.

Alignment. Orcs tend toward lawful evil, half-orcs tend toward true neutral. PC orcs and half-orcs may be of any alignment.

Natural Armor Class. Orcs and half-orcs have natural armor classes of 10.

Background. Orcs look like primitive humans with gray-green skin and coarse hair. They stoop slightly, have low jutting foreheads,

snouts, canine-like teeth, and short pointed ears. The average orc stands between 5½ and 6 feet tall. Half orcs have much more human features.

Orcs are aggressive humanoids that live in tribal societies. They band together to hunt and raid, believing that to survive they must expand their territory. This need to expand puts them in a constant state of war with humans, elves, dwarves, goblins, and even other orc tribes.

Orc communities are usually found underground (75% likely), but wilderness villages do exist. These lairs are protected by the best defenses the orcs can invent or steal. Some of these communities are built around active mines. All make use of slave labor.

The orc mentality views aggression as the natural order. They believe that other races are inferior to them, and bully weaker creatures. Enslaved orcs will rebel at the first opportunity. When allied with others, orcs are quick to take offense and break agreements.

To orcs, the greatest challenge they can set for themselves is the test of battle. They value territory above all else, though they also take great pride in battle experience and prowess, wealth, and lots of offspring. Orc society is male dominated; females exist to bear young. Though carnivorous, orcs prefer game meats or livestock to intelligent races.

Half-Orcs: Half-orcs result from orc unions with virtually any humanoid or demihuman race except elves. These mixed breeds tend to favor their orcish parent, though a small number can pass for ugly humans. PC half orcs are assumed to be crossbreeds within the upper 10% of the mongrel orc-humans that can pass for human. These have the ability to surpass their orcish heritage, rising beyond the limits a normal orc can reach. However, they have difficulty finding a place in either society, as neither culture trusts them.

Languages. Orc, goblin, hobgoblin, ogre, common. Half-orcs speak orc and receive common as a bonus language.

Role-Playing Suggestions. Player character orcs are not as rare as other humanoid races. The call to battle is not much different than the call to adventure, and orc heroes sometimes come to the forefront. If treated with care and patience, orc adventurers can become effective partners and allies. Because females have few rights in orc society, many of them turn to adventuring to escape their lot in life.

A few orcs even attempt to reject their evil natures in order to try to become honorable warriors. While an orc will never become a paladin, some do attain the orcish equivalent of holy warriors. However, those orcs that attempt to fight fair and with honor are sneered at and rejected by their own kind. Why fight face to face, the common orc thinks, when fighting from an advantageous hiding place is so much more effective?

Half-orcs: Half-orcs have an easier time of it as adventurers, for they are usually free of tribal ties. Both heritages reject them, so they must carve their own destiny out of what life

throws their way. They often flaunt their superior ability in the presence of full orcs, and tend to associate with humans who do not care about appearances.

Half-orcs tend to be serious and brooding. They seek acceptance and friendship, even though most will have little to do with them. While most of the half-breeds walk the path of neutrality, a few do become lawful good.

Special Advantages. Orcs (only) are skilled miners. They can spot new and unusual constructions 35% of the time, and sloping passages 25% of the time.

Orcs and half orcs have 60-foot infravision.

Half-orc single classed characters with exceptional ability scores can advance further: Fighter 17th at 21 Strength (20—14th; 19—12th; 18/00—11th). Priests gain one level per point of Wisdom up to 7th level. Thieves gain one level per point of Dexterity up to 11th level.

Special Disadvantages. Orcs fight with a –1 penalty to their attack rolls and morale when in direct sunlight. Half-orcs do not have this disadvantage.

Monstrous Traits. Appearance.

Superstitions. Fear of sickness, the weak, the lame, cowards, sunlight.

Weapon Proficiencies: Battle axe, crossbow, flail, hand axe, spear, any bow, any pole arm, any sword.

Nonweapon Proficiencies: Alertness, armorer, blacksmithing, bowyer/fletcher, carpentry, chanting, close-quarter fighting, hunting, intimidation, looting, religion, set snares, spellcraft, tracking, weaponsmithing.

Pixie

Ability Score Adjustments. The initial ability scores are modified by a +1 bonus to Dexterity and Charisma, and a –1 penalty to Strength and Constitution.

Ability Score Range

Ability	Minimum	Maximum
Strength	3	14
Dexterity	8	19
Constitution	7	16
Intelligence	6	18
Wisdom	3	16
Charisma	3	18

Class Restrictions

Class	Maximum Level
Warrior	
Fighter	7
Ranger	—
Paladin	—
Wizard	
Mage	—
Illusionist	—
Priest	
Cleric	—
Druid	—
Shaman	—
Witch Doctor	—
Rogue	
Thief	12
Bard	—

Hit Dice. Player character pixies receive hit dice by class.

Alignment. Pixies are true neutral. PC pixies can be any neutral alignment.

Natural Armor Class. 5.

Background. Pixies are among the most intelligent and mischievous of the magical faerie-kind. They dwell in idyllic woodlands, taking great delight in harassing travelers with their pranks and tricks. Fun is the goal for nearly all pixies, and they often define fun by the merry pranks they pull.

Pixies are naturally invisible. When they make themselves visible, they look like two and a half foot tall elves, though their pointed ears are much longer. The silver moth wings jutting from their backs gives them the ability

to fly. They dress in bright colors, often sporting caps and shoes with curled, pointed toes.

These elfin beings inhabit deep forest caves. They dance in moonlit glades, moving to the music of crickets, frogs, and other nocturnal creatures. They live in clans or family units that seem to mimic human customs. If they take anything seriously, it is their loyalty to family and community.

They also take great pride in their martial skills. They can appear warlike, and they love to play at adventure as much as they love trickery and celebration.

Languages. Pixie, sprite, common.

Role-Playing Suggestions. Pixie PCs often join up with adventurers who display a good sense of humor (especially if they were on the receiving end of a pixie prank). With childlike wonder and a sense of adventure, pixies will take up sword and bow and follow other characters on important missions and grand quests. No matter how serious the quest is, however, pixies always treat it as a game.

Even when on an adventure, they cannot refrain from pulling pranks on monsters and other creatures they meet. If no one else is available, they may even turn their tricks on their companions. If they see a young maiden, they must frighten her. If they find a wall, they must rap upon it. No candle flame is safe in the presence of a pixie, and no inviting frog pond or flower field can be ignored.

Pixies may play tricks to teach lessons, greedy misers and humorless bores are prime targets. Most often, they play tricks for the sheer fun of it. They love celebrations and feasts, and are often considered frivolous by the larger races. They are graceful, with a love for life. Pixies loathe evil, saving their most lethal tricks for foul bandits and wicked monsters. When they need an item, they have no second thoughts about "borrowing" it.

Pixies can be played for comic relief, but their abilities with weapons makes them more than simple pranksters. They can become valuable members of any adventuring party.

Special Advantages. Pixies can become visible or polymorph themselves at will. Once per day they can *know alignment*.

Once per day a pixie can *create illusions* with both auditory and visual components, which last without concentration until dispelled.

Once per day pixies can touch a creature or being and cause *confusion* (as the spell) if the creature fails a saving throw vs. spells. This confusion is permanent unless a *remove curse* is applied or the pixie dispels it.

Once per day, pixies can use *dispel magic* (as an 8th level mage), *dancing lights*, and *ESP*.

Opponents who cannot detect invisible objects attack pixies with a –4 penalty. Pixies can attack while invisible without penalty.

Pixies have the ability to fly, with a movement speed of 12 and a maneuverability of B.

Special Disadvantages. A *dispel magic* successful against 8th level magic will force a pixie to become visible for one round.

A pixie requires *twice* as much XP to advance a level as a human of the same class.

Monstrous Traits. Size, invisibility, wings.

Superstitions. Pixies avoid stagnant, filthy

pools of water, seeing them as bad omens or manifestations of evil.

Weapon Proficiencies: Dagger, *pixie bow, pixie sword.*

Nonweapon Proficiencies: Animal lore, animal noises, bowyer/fletcher, brewing, cheesemaking, direction sense, fast-talking, gaming, hiding, observation, set snares, ventriloquism, voice mimicry, weaponsmithing, winemaking.

Satyr

Ability Score Adjustments. The initial ability scores are modified by a +1 bonus to Dexterity and Constitution, and a –1 penalty to Intelligence and Charisma.

Ability Score Range

Ability	Minimum	Maximum
Strength	6	18/75
Dexterity	8	18
Constitution	7	18
Intelligence	3	17
Wisdom	3	18
Charisma	3	17

Class Restrictions

Class	Maximum Level
Warrior	
Fighter	11
Ranger	7
Paladin	—
Wizard	
Mage	—
Illusionist	—
Priest	
Cleric	—
Druid	—
Shaman	—
Witch Doctor	—
Rogue	
Thief	11
Bard	—

Hit Dice. Player character satyrs receive hit dice by class.

Alignment. Satyrs are true neutral. PC satyrs can be any alignment.

Natural Armor Class. 5.

Background. The half-human, half-goat satyrs are a race of pleasure-loving beings. Like the sylvan locations they dwell in, satyrs are personifications of nature, embodiments of all that is wild and carefree.

Satyrs, also called fauns, have the torso, head and arms of a man, and the hind legs of a goat. Two sharp black horns jut through the coarse, curly hair on top of the head.

Satyrs spend their days and nights in sport. They love to frolic and play their pipes, and they never miss an opportunity to chase after wood nymphs or other comely creatures. While they can be friendly to strangers, they usually resent intrusion into their territory. They get along best with elves, centaurs, and dryads, and occasionally mingle with korred.

These fun-loving creatures often throw wild woodland celebrations. During the warmer periods of the year, these celebrations can last all night. They are attended by dryads, cen-

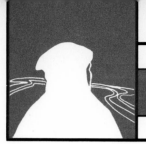

taurs, and other woodland creatures. Strangers who stumble onto such a party will be invited to stay if they can supply drink. Satyrs are extremely fond of expensive wine.

Satyrs refuse to confine themselves to an organized society. They live in loose colonies, instead, using comfortable caves and hollow trees as homes. There are no female satyrs. They do have an affection for human females, however, and often seek to charm those that catch their fancy.

Languages. Satyr, sylvan elf, centaur, dryad, korred (rare), common.

Role-Playing Suggestions. Satyrs are an inoffensive race. They just want to have fun. The rare satyr who becomes an adventurer often does so for the sport of it. When adventures stop being fun, they return to their woodland homes to find a new party.

Satyrs do not understand seriousness or violence. Though they can fight with the best of them if need be, they are rarely serious. It's against their nature. They do not like to work (though they are excellent wine makers), as their hearts are tuned to play. They are impulsive, full of animal passions. If they see something they like, then they must have it immediately. To want is to get, at least in the mind of a typical satyr.

They believe themselves to be part of nature, an extension of its wild side. As such, the satyr way is nature's way — the right way. They are not thinkers, preferring instead to live in the now. Why contemplate a plan? Just get on with it, or don't. That's the satyr's way. Also, satyrs do not get angry or insulted. Everything is the way it is, so why should they be bothered by it?

Satyr PCs will often be unpredictable, as the object of their desire changes from moment to moment, and they are quick to act on their impulses. They understand that humans and demihumans think differently than they do, and they can suppress some of their urges. However, satyrs will be quick to point out how absurd it is to try to keep a reign on feelings, and may even attempt to teach their companions how to loosen up and have fun.

Special Advantages. Because of their ability to be very silent and their keen senses, satyrs are surprised only on a roll of 1.

In forest settings, satyrs can blend into the foliage (90% undetectable to creatures who cannot see hidden or invisible things).

Satyrs have infravision to 60 feet.

In melee, satyrs can head butt for 2-8 points of damage instead of using weapons.

If a satyr has constructed his own satyr pipe, and has devoted a minimum of three proficiency slots to its use (musical instrument, pipes) he can use its music to either *charm* or *sleep* or *cause fear* to all within 60 feet. All who hear the pipes must make a successful saving throw vs. spell or suffer the effect. No proficiency check is required to use the pipes in this manner. A bard's singing can nullify the music of a satyr pipe.

Special Disadvantages. Satyrs are very susceptible to distraction, especially if this comes from a female with Charisma 15 or better or from an expensive bottle of wine.

Monstrous Traits. Appearance.

Superstitions. Satyrs are uncomfortable in cities and beneath the ground, they do not like mobs of humans or humanoids, and fear boredom most of all.

Weapon Proficiencies: Dagger, javelin, long sword, short sword, short bow, spear.

Nonweapon Proficiencies: Acting, alertness, animal lore, artistic ability, bowyer/fletcher, brewing, cheesemaking, craft instrument (satyr pipe), dancing, drinking, eating, fishing, gaming, hiding, hunting, juggling, musical instrument (satyr pipe), natural fighting, poetry, survival (forest), whistling/humming, winemaking.

Saurial

Ability Score Adjustments. The initial ability scores are modified as follows:
- *Bladeback:* +1 Wis, +1 Cha; –2 Dex
- *Finhead:* no bonus or penalty
- *Flyer:* +2 Dex; –1 Str, –1 Con
- *Hornhead:* +1 Str, +1 Int; –2 Dex

Ability Score Range

Ability	Minimum (bb/fn/fl/hh)	Maximum (bb/fn/fl/hh)
Strength	10/7/3/12	18/18/17/18
Dexterity	3/5/7/2	14/18/19/12
Constitution	5/3/3/8	18/18/17/18
Intelligence	3/3/3/7	18/18/18/19
Wisdom	7/3/3/3	18/18/18/18
Charisma	5/3/3/3	18/18/18/18

Class Restrictions

Class	Maximum Level* (bb/fh/fl/hh)
Warrior	
Fighter	9/U/9/9
Ranger	—/12/—/—
Paladin	—/12/—/—
Wizard	
Mage	9/9/9/U
Illusionist	—/—/—/12
Priest	
Cleric	U/9/9/9
Druid	9/9/9/9
Shaman	—/—/—/—
Witch Doctor	—/—/—/—
Rogue	
Thief	9/9/U/9
Bard	—/—/—/—

* If ability scores allow an XP bonus, then a 9 maximum becomes a 10 maximum. These maximums are theoretical based on the small sample available for study.

Hit Dice. Player character saurials receive hit dice by class. In addition bladebacks receive 2 bonus hit points at first level and hornheads receive 4 bonus hit points.

Alignment. Saurial characters can be of any alignment.

Natural Armor Class. Flyers have a natural armor class of 6, finheads 5, and bladebacks and hornheads 4.

Background. The saurials are a race of lizard people who come from an alternate Prime Material plane. To date they have only appeared in the Realms, having been kidnapped and brought there by the evil god Moander. When the god died, the saurials decided to make the Realms their home.

Saurials are intelligent bipedal lizards that appear to be descended from creatures much like dinosaurs. Those in the Realms live in a single village in the Lost Vale, among the peaks of the Desertsmouth Mountains east of Anauroch. Most are still recovering from the physical, mental and spiritual anguish they suffered as Moander's slaves, and few venture out of the safety of their valley.

There are many different races of saurials, but only four are currently in the Realms. These are the bladebacks, finheads, flyers, and hornheads — names given them by the natives of the Realms. Their own names are a combination of noises and scents that do not translate into human or humanoid speech.

Saurials have brightly colored scales, sharp claws, and tails. The different races have much different body shapes. All, however, are roughly humanoid. Bladebacks are tall, standing about seven feet, with stocky frames and friendly faces. The name given them comes from their most prominent physical feature. Large, sharp scales jut out along their spines, extending from the tops of their heads to the end of their almost body-length tails. Finheads are closest in shape to humans, though slightly shorter, standing about five feet tall. A pronounced fin sweeps from this saurial's head, and it has a tail that is a little more than half the length of its body. Flyers are small,

averaging just three feet in height. They have delicate frames, small legs, short tails, and flaps of scale-covered skin hanging from each arm. This skin serves as wings, giving these saurials the ability to fly. Hornheads are the largest of the saurials, standing 10 feet tall with tails that stretch longer than their bodies. Sharp horns protrude from their heads and the great bony plates at their necks, giving this saurial race its name. All saurials come in shades of green mixed with yellow patterns, while flyers sometimes sport red splotches. Rarely, a pure white saurial is born to one of the races.

More than one hundred adult saurials live in the Lost Vale. They consider themselves to be of one tribe. Most of the saurials are farmers and hunters, though a small number of young saurials are becoming adventurers. Saurials think of themselves as saurials first and their sub-race second. They mate for life, live a long time, and both males and females share equally in all work.

Saurial magic-users use memory sticks instead of spellbooks. These notched poles function like human spellbooks, though they are sometimes mistaken for magical staves by those unfamiliar with saurial customs.

Languages. Saurials cannot speak any human or humanoid language. Their voices are pitched too high for humans to hear, though the olfactory portion of their own language can be detected. They emit scents which carry their emotions, and these can be interpreted by humans familiar with saurials. Those saurials who are PC adventurers usually have some magical item that allows them to communicate with their non-saurial companions.

Role-Playing Suggestions. As time goes on, saurial adventurers like Dragonbait™ will become more common. The inhabitants of the Lost Vale will decide to venture out, and it is possible that others from their home plane may find their ways to the Realms and other campaign worlds.

Those adults in the Lost Vale are a somber lot, hoping the next generation of offspring will bring joy back to their lives. Only the finhead named Dragonbait is known to have taken up adventuring, but the stories he brings back to the valley on his visits have begun to inspire other saurials.

Young saurials grow quickly, reaching adult size in about five years. However, they take as long as humans to mature mentally and socially, so very young saurial PCs could be played as large children who still have a lot of growing up to do. Perhaps they have run away from the Lost Vale, their heads filled with the tales of Dragonbait. Older saurials could leave the valley on some quest, to get away from the somber mood that hangs over the community, or could even be from their home plane on a mission to find their lost brethren.

Bladebacks are very social beings. They enjoy company, and always find time to socialize. They are the most straight-forward and trusting of the saurial races, but they also understand saurial nature well enough to know the motives and desires of the other races. Slow to anger, bladebacks become passionate fighters when finally roused to battle. They have very long memories, which makes them slow to forgive insults and offenses. Bladebacks tend to be leaders and advisors, and many become priests so they can tend to the needs of the community.

Finheads tend to be alert, bright, active, curious and highly emotional. They often become fighters. Most believe in ultimate good and evil, seeing things in terms of black and white. To finheads, there is one truth — they tend to defend that truth with every muscle in their bodies. New tasks and adventures are greeted enthusiastically. Being impulsive, they often leap into dangerous situations without fully understanding what they are up against. Finheads are the most likely to leave the community to seek out adventure.

Flyers are nervous and skittish. On the ground they are clumsy and ill at ease. In the air, they are graceful and fluid. They are easily irritated and in turn can be very irritating. They are full of nervous energy, constantly on the move and bouncing around. They love to talk, constantly chattering about gossip and any topic that comes to mind. They are nosy, often snooping on companions just so they can keep tabs on everything that is going on. Flyers act as scouts and messengers.

Flyers flee when danger presents itself. This is done almost on reflex, though they will return if they are needed in a fight. Every flyer knows in the back of his mind that their companions need them, and they often make up stories wherein they save the day for their larger companions. They love to tell these stories over and over again — even if they have no basis in fact.

Hornheads are careful planners and rational thinkers. They never rush into anything. Sometimes they seem dim-witted because they speak slowly and always choose their words with extreme care. Their minds, however, are sharp and quick, and hornheads often take up science and crafts. They make natural wizards. For all their size and strength, they are among the most peace-loving of the saurials. They are not motivated to demonstrate their own strength and power at every occasion. Because of their great size, hornheads can often be found eating. They require a lot of vegetation to maintain their strength.

Many saurials, especially spellcasters, decorate themselves with intricate tattoos which are carved into their scales or bony plates. Though they cannot speak common, some can understand it. They usually do not announce this fact to everyone, preferring the advantage they gain by appearing to be less intelligent than they really are.

Special Advantages. All saurials have infravision to 60 feet.

If necessary, saurials can use their ancient fighting methods. Bladebacks claw twice (1d4 damage each) and swing their razored tails at rear attackers (1d6). Finheads have claws (1d3/1d3) and their whip tail (1d2). Flyers employ their claws and bite (1d2/1d2, 1d2). Hornheads use claws (1d4/1d4), their tail (2d4), can charge with their horns (2d6).

All saurials receive a +2 saving throw bonus against sound-based attacks (such as a harpy *charm* or a *shout* spell).

Flyers fly at a speed of 24 and have a maneuver class of C.

Special Disadvantages. Saurials do not get percentile ratings for Strength regardless of class. Saurial wizards cannot use other races' spell books or scrolls.

Saurials forced to use non-saurial weapons suffer a –1 attack penalty.

Gas- or scent-based attacks, such as poison gas and *stinking cloud* spells, have a greater effect on saurials. They receive a –2 penalty to saving throws against these attacks.

Bladebacks and hornheads take damage as large creatures.

If exposed to prolonged cold, saurials fall into a torpor called *cold sleep*. They can resist this for a number of turns equal to their size (flyers, 3 turns; hornheads 10 turns). Times can be doubled if they wear insulated clothing. Warmth revives them one to two hours. More than a day in the cold causes death.

Monstrous Traits. Appearance, size, method of speech.

Superstitions. Saurials fear evil gods due to the treatment they endured under Moander.

Weapon Proficiencies: Any *saurial weapons* usable by their class are allowed. Fighters can become proficient in non-saurial weapons.

Nonweapon Proficiencies: Any usable by their class.

Swanmay

Ability Score Adjustments. The initial ability scores are modified by a +1 bonus to Dexterity and Wisdom.

Ability Score Range

Ability	Minimum*	Maximum
Strength	13/9	18
Dexterity	13/9	18
Constitution	14/12	18
Intelligence	9/12	18
Wisdom	14/12	19
Charisma	9/15	18

* The second number is for the druid class. These ability score minimums include the class minimums.

Class Restrictions

Class	Maximum Level
Warrior	
Fighter	—
Ranger	14
Paladin	—
Wizard	
Mage	—
Illusionist	—
Priest	
Cleric	—
Druid	12
Shaman	—
Witch Doctor	—
Rogue	
Thief	—
Bard	—

Hit Dice. Player character swanmays receive hit dice by class.

Alignment. Swanmays have the alignment of their class, either any good (ranger) or true neutral (druid).

Natural Armor Class. 7.

Background. Swanmays are human females who can transform into swans (but they are not actually swans). In human form, they are indistinguishable from other people, appear-

ing by their garb and equipment much like rangers or druids. When they shift into swan form, their equipment remains behind. Thus, swanmays try to hide these items before undergoing transformation.

Swanmays belong to a special sorority of shapechanging rangers and druids. Their ability to transform into swans at will is granted by the special token they carry (which only functions for them). This may be feather token, a feathered garment, a signet ring, etc. The token transforms into part of the swan's plumage or appears on the transformed swan's leg. These magical tokens can be spotted by use of a *detect magic* spell.

The swanmay sorority is very secretive. Only human females are admitted, usually after they have unknowingly preformed a great service for another swanmay. Most retire from casual adventuring to devote themselves full time to their new responsibilities.

Swanmays live in communal lodges near bodies of water in hidden forests. They hate poachers and others who disturb the natural order of the land. They dislike brash, noisy creatures, ferocious beasts, and monsters of

evil alignment. They are friends and protectors of the forest folk, though they tend to avoid other humanoids. Swanmays might approach nature-oriented priests or close adventuring companions when they require assistance against some great evil.

Languages. Sylvan elf, dryad, common.

Role-Playing Suggestions. Swanmays are independent protectors of the forests and wildlife. PC swanmays should try to make sure that their adventuring actively opposes evil races and monsters that despoil the wildlife and countryside.

Swanmays rarely, if ever, reveal their true natures —even to close companions. Even if their natures are known, they will reveal nothing about the sorority they belong to. They seek adventures that will ultimately benefit nature, the wetlands, and the forests.

Special Advantages. All special advantages apply in swan form only. A swanmay can only be harmed by +1 weapons or better. Swanmays have an innate magic resistance of 2% per hit die. The swanmay can fly at a speed of 19, maneuverability class D.

Special Disadvantages. Without their special tokens, swanmays are trapped in their current form. If the token is stolen, the swanmay cannot change until it is recovered. If the token is destroyed, the swanmay must go on a special quest in order to replace it.

Monstrous Traits. Transformation ability.

Superstitions. Swanmays watch nature for signs and omens. Their deep hatred of all things evil may sometimes approach fear.

Weapon Proficiencies: Broad sword, dagger, long bow, long sword, short bow, short sword.

Nonweapon Proficiencies: Alertness, animal handling, animal lore, animal noise, bowyer/fletcher, danger sense, direction sense, firebuilding, fishing, hiding, hunting, set snares, survival (forests, wetlands), swimming,

Bonus Proficiencies: Ranger — tracking, druid — weather sense.

Wemic

Ability Score Adjustments. The initial ability scores are modified by a +1 bonus to Strength and a –1 penalty to Dexterity.

Ability Score Range

Ability	Minimum	Maximum
Strength	11	18
Dexterity	6	17
Constitution	11	18
Intelligence	3	18
Wisdom	3	18
Charisma	3	18

Class Restrictions

Class	Maximum Level
Warrior	
Fighter	12
Ranger	—
Paladin	—
Wizard	
Mage	—
Illusionist	—
Priest	
Cleric	—
Druid	—
Shaman	7
Witch Doctor	7
Rogue	
Thief	—
Bard	10

Hit Dice. Player character wemics receive hit dice by class. In addition they receive 5 bonus hit points at first level.

Alignment. Most wemics are neutral. PC wemics can be of any alignment.

Natural Armor Class. 6.

Background. Wemics are part human, part lion, combining the two as centaurs combine human and horse. The wemic's leonine body has a human torso extending from what would be a lion's neck. Wemics grow to 10 feet long,

reaching heights of six to seven feet when standing erect.

The leonine body is covered with dusky golden fur, while the underbelly fur is short and white. The tip of the tail is a brush of long black hair, and adult males also have a flowing mane of long black hair. The face is leonine, and the eyes are usually golden with slit pupils. The claws of the forepaws are retractable, the hind claws are not.

Wemics blend leonine and aboriginal human cultures in a primitive society. They live in nomadic groups called "prides", surviving through hunting. They know and use fire, and craft stone weaponry, pottery, and ornaments. Wemics have human intelligence; if exposed to more complex skills they can learn, providing they can overcome their superstitious nature.

Witch doctors and shamans are very important to wemic society, for the primitive hunters see everything as supernatural. Weather and the changing of day into night are functions of the gods. Everything is personified and alive and magical — the sun, the moon, the clouds, the rivers. Such is how wemics see the world.

Languages. Wemic, common.

Role-Playing Suggestions. Wemics are playful and curious as cubs, and they keep these traits into adulthood. They are excellent hunters, trackers, and guides, often hiring themselves out in exchange for treasure, tools, and magical items. This is one way for a wemic to come into contact with an adventuring party. Others are captured as cubs and raised as servants or slaves. PC wemics can be either recently freed, or can be free wemics who have left home to explore the world.

The primitive wemics risk exploitation by more advanced societies. They are taken as slaves, cheated into servitude, or even tricked out of valuable items they do not understand.

Wemics have a great deal of pride and courage — except against obvious agents of the supernatural. If they cannot defeat a foe with weapon or claws, then that foe cannot be

defeated. They are noble savages, with honor and compassion. Once they alley themselves to a group or cause, they stick with it to the end.

Special Advantages. Wemics can attack with both foreleg claws for 1-4 points of damage each. They can also attack with hand-held weapons at the same time.

These leonine creatures have powerful leg muscles which allow them to leap 10 feet upward or 30 feet forward.

Special Disadvantages. Wemics take damage as large creatures.

Monstrous Traits. Appearance.

Superstitions. All of nature is personified in the wemic's mind, and thus every whisper of wind and rumble of earth is an omen. Certain modern items frighten them until they learn what they are. They especially fear obviously supernatural beings and the undead.

Weapon Proficiencies: Club (stone), javelin, short sword, spear.

Nonweapon Proficiencies: Animal noise, eating, fire-building, hunting, natural fighting, religion, spellcraft, survival (plains), tracking, weaponsmithing, weaving, wild fighting.

CHAPTER

3

Humanoid Kits

This chapter describes the humanoid kits for every class. The use of these kits, while optional, is recommended. Table 8: Character Kit Summary provides a quick reference list of which humanoids and classes are eligible for which kits.

All of the kits in this book are designed for humanoids. Because each humanoid race is so different, the kits are defined in broad terms. When matching a humanoid to a kit, be sure to add the details from the humanoid's entry (in Chapter Two) to the kit information when setting up your character sheet.

Dungeon Masters may allow their players to use kits from the *PHBR* rules supplements with their humanoid characters. While this is not recommended when first introducing humanoid PCs into a campaign, it certainly can be explored at a later date. When starting out, the special kits in this chapter are the best way to create humanoid player characters.

Proficiencies

Kits use the proficiency rules outlined in Chapter 5 of the *Player's Handbook*. If you are using kits, then these rules are not optional. Be sure to review them before selecting a humanoid kit. Unless otherwise noted, all humanoids will receive the number of proficiency slots given to their class according to Table 34 in the *Player's Handbook*.

Kit Descriptions

Each kit begins with a brief overview. This gives a quick sketch of the type of character it can be used to create. Other sections within each kit include the following:

Requirements: This section lists which humanoids are definitely eligible for the kit and which ones are not. If a particular race is not mentioned, it should only be selected after consultation with the Dungeon Master. This section also notes whether or not both males

and females can use the kit, and lists any alignment requirements that might exist.

Role: This section provides more details on a character's place in both human and humanoid society. It describes how most of the typical members of the kit will act. Player characters are not required to follow this information to the letter.

Weapon Proficiencies: Some kits indicate that specific weapon proficiencies must be taken when the character is created. These cost the usual number of proficiency slots as outlined in the *Player's Handbook*. Otherwise, use the standard class guidelines.

Nonweapon Proficiencies: Some kits also require certain nonweapon proficiencies. There are several types of proficiencies that a kit might have. First are *bonus* proficiencies. These are free proficiencies requiring no proficiency slots. Second are *required* proficiencies. These must be taken and require proficiency slots. Third are *recommended* proficiencies. These are optional and cost the usual number of slots. Recommended proficiencies are organized by group — general, warrior, priest, wizard, and rogue. When a player selects a proficiency from the groups listed for the character's class, it costs the usual number of slots. Selecting a proficiency from any other category costs one additional slot unless a specific kit states otherwise. Table 38 from the chapter of the *Player's Handbook* on proficiencies has been reprinted here for convenience.

Note: There are new humanoid proficiencies for each group, as well as some important restrictions concerning proficiencies from the *Player's Handbook* and the *PHBR* series (see Chapter Four for more information).

Finally, an entry might include *forbidden* proficiencies. These cannot be chosen by a character who adopts the kit. Later, if there are campaign reasons why a character might acquire a forbidden proficiency, the DM may choose whether or not to allow it.

Equipment: Restrictions on a kit's use of weapons and armor are listed here. This limits the character to the weapons and armor typically used by other characters employing the same kit.

Special Benefits: Almost every kit includes a special advantage that sets its members apart from members of other kits. These could be combat benefits, reaction adjustments, or learning advantages. Many involve a bonus to encounter reactions (see Table 59 in the *Dungeon Master™ Guide*, Chapter 11).

Important Note: All bonuses are expressed as positive numbers, and penalties as negative numbers. Thus, if a low number is good for the character, a bonus is actually *subtracted* from the die roll and a penalty is *added*. Some benefits include individual class awards (see Chapter 8 in the *DMG*).

Magical Abilities: This section applies only to priests. It lists spheres of access, special benefits for spell use, and forbidden spells. The ability (or inability) to turn or command undead is also noted here.

Special Hindrances: Like benefits, these are usually unique to each character kit. They often force or prohibit certain actions.

Wealth Options: A character's starting funds are explained here. Note that in general humanoid characters start with considerably less funds than their human and demihuman counterparts.

Table 3: Nonweapon Proficiency Group Crossovers

Character Class	Proficiency Groups
Fighter	Warrior, General
Paladin	Warrior, Priest, General
Ranger	Warrior, Wizard, General
Cleric	Priest, General
Druid	Priest, Warrior, General
Mage	Wizard, General
Illusionist	Wizard, General
Thief	Rogue, General
Bard	Rogue, Warrior, Wizard, General

Warrior Kits

The most common kits used by humanoid characters are the warrior kits. From the semi-organized military training sessions of the goblins and hobgoblins to the humanoid races which learn to fight simply through daily survival, warrior humanoids are everywhere. As most humanoids can only select the fighter class in the warrior group, the kits which follow all belong to that category — with two exceptions. There are two kits which simulate the paladin and ranger classes. Those few humanoid races which can choose these classes *must* take the appropriate kit to simulate the abilities of paladins and rangers. Here is an overview of the humanoid warrior kits:

- *Tribal defenders* protect their tribe's territory from all invaders. These warriors represent the typical fighters of a given race. They have the fewest hindrances, and the fewest special abilities.
- *Mine rowdies* are fighters specially trained to fight in underground or enclosed areas. They are proficient in subterranean survival skills and close-quarters fighting.
- *Pit fighters* have been trained to fight for the amusement of others. In some cases, their training comes not from their masters but from the simple act of surviving battle after battle.
- *Sellswords* hire themselves out to others. They act as guards, mercenaries, bounty hunters, and swords-for-hire, taking on any job which requires fighting skills and muscle. This kit is the closest one to a true professional warrior a humanoid can have.
- *Saurial paladins* are holy saurial warriors — the equivalent of human paladins. This kit is open only to saurials, like Dragonbait of the Forgotten Realms.
- *Wilderness protectors* are much like rangers, with abilities similar to their human and demihuman counterparts.

Tribal Defender

Tribal defenders are the most common humanoid warriors. Every humanoid tribe, settlement, clan, and family group must be protected from the dangers of the world, and these proud warriors are the backbone of every tribe's defense. Some humanoid races organize true armies or militias, but most simply place their safety in the hands of the strongest, most able-bodied tribe members.

Player character tribal defenders have left their tribes for some reason (usually the character's primary motivation). They take with them whatever skills they learned while protecting their tribes, but now they use these skills to ensure their own survival.

Requirements: None, other than those listed in the humanoid race entries (for example, female bugbears would not be tribal defenders, as they do not fight unless absolutely necessary). All humanoid races have tribal defenders, these can be of any alignment.

Role: Tribal defenders are humanoids with fighting skills. All tribe members who are not restricted by sexual bias or relegated to other tasks (because of abilities or circumstances) are taught to fight for the tribe.

Tribal defenders are rarely thinkers. Some are full-time soldiers who protect the tribe and territory. Others are part-time warriors who take up club and spear when danger threatens. The more organized the race, the better trained the defender is. A rare few develop heroic abilities after long years of warfare or constant training, as dictated by the character's background history. In most humanoid tribes, tribal defenders can eventually rise to positions of power and leadership, since many races have a high regard for martial prowess.

Most tribes do not grant special privileges to the tribal defender. These fighters are only doing their part for the survival of the tribe. However, defenders who leave their tribes to chase some crazy dream or quest, or to escape their lot in life, are often considered cowards, traitors, and outcasts. They are hated, sometimes hunted, and always shunned.

Other races are most familiar with humanoid tribal defenders as opposed to other humanoid kits, for these are the warriors they most often find themselves competing with. Reactions to tribal defenders depend upon the humanoid race in question and the race of those they meet. Most are hated, especially by those races usually at odds with them.

Weapon Proficiencies: Members of this kit must spend all of their initial weapon proficiency slots on weapons available to their race.

Nonweapon Proficiencies:

• Required Proficiencies: Hunting or agriculture.

• Recommended, General: Animal noise, animal training (tribal guard animal), blacksmithing, direction sense, fire-building, fishing, leatherworking, mining, observation.

• Recommended, Warrior: Bowyer/fletcher, endurance, gaming, intimidation, natural fighting, set snares, weaponsmithing.

• Recommended, Rogue: Information gathering, local history (tribal).

• Forbidden: Wild fighting.

Equipment: Tribal defenders should choose weapons and armor typical of their culture. Use common sense to decide what would be usable and available to adventuring tribal defenders.

Special Benefits: After long years defending a particular territory, the character is intimately familiar with it. The player and his DM should determine where the humanoid's original territory is located, and any proficiency checks made in the area in regards to interacting with the area and its inhabitants receive a +2 bonus.

Special Hindrances: On the other hand, departed tribal defender PCs are no longer welcomed in their original territory. Campaign complication checks should be made more frequently if they return (see Chapter Five).

Wealth Options: Tribal defenders begin play with 5d4 × 5 gp.

Mine Rowdy

Mine rowdies are fighters trained to keep order and defend mines and other underground work areas. They are tough, intimidating overseers who are fast to squelch fights, quick to give orders, and ready to wade into any danger to carry out the job that has been given them. These roughnecks keep mine workers productive and focused, whether those workers are members of the tribe or slaves in the tribe's thrall. Every mine rowdy is responsible to oversee and protect that portion of a mine placed in his care. Any failure can lead to banishment, hard labor, or even death.

Player character mine rowdies have usually left their lairs in order to escape punishment due to some failure on their part. Perhaps a rowdy is the only survivor of a collapsed mine or a mine that was overrun by hostile forces. Maybe productivity dropped sharply and the rowdy was stripped of his position. Maybe the slaves and workers in his charge rebelled, and the rowdy had to flee in order to escape their wrath or the wrath of the tribe's leaders. Or maybe a rowdy, tired of being cruel and overbearing, showed compassion to those laboring for him or even set some slaves free. This simple action immediately made him a traitor and outcast among his own kind.

Requirements: Mine rowdies must come from races that labor beneath the ground or keep slaves that do. Of those humanoids detailed in this book, the following may select this kit: bugbears, gnolls, flinds, hobgoblins, half-ogres, minotaurs, orcs, and half-orcs. Mine rowdies must have a minimum Strength of 15 and can be of any alignment.

Role: Among those humanoids who make lairs or labor beneath the earth, the role of mine rowdy is well known. It takes vast numbers of workers and slaves to mine ore and dig tunnels and lairs. Someone must supervise these workers, keep them motivated, and make sure nothing delays productivity. That's where mine rowdies come in.

Rowdies are strong, cruel, and demanding taskmasters. A rowdy has been given a sacred duty by his chief or shaman, and that duty is never taken lightly. When slaves refuse to work or threaten to revolt, the mine rowdy appears to put them back in their place. When tribal laborers grow lazy, the mine rowdy uses muscle and intimidation to motivate them. When subterranean dangers invade the work areas, the rowdy leaps to protect the area, taking his place at the forefront of any defenders under his command.

Members of this kit are tough, brave, forceful, and quick to action. They are used to being in command, and often throw their weight around even among their adventuring companions. If a job has to be done, they take it upon themselves to make sure the work proceeds. They have extremely developed work ethics.

Player character rowdies have lost honor and position in their tribes. They are forced to leave the lairs they knew behind to make a life in the larger world. They make useful allies because of their skills in underground regions and their fighting prowess.

Weapon Proficiencies: Mine rowdies must take one bludgeoning weapon and one piercing weapon as part of their initial weapon proficiencies.

Nonweapon Proficiencies:
• Required Proficiencies: Intimidation.
• Recommended, General: Chanting, danger sense, direction sense (underground), mining.
• Recommended, Warrior: Close-quarter fighting, endurance, gaming, survival (underground), wild fighting.
• Recommended, Priest: Engineering.
• Recommended, Rogue: Appraising (ore/gems only), gem cutting.
• Forbidden: Agriculture, hiding, survival (any except underground), weather sense. Note: These proficiencies are forbidden initially, but may be learned by the mine rowdy, should the opportunity for learning these proficiencies arise.

Equipment: Rowdies cannot begin play with armor heavier than chain mail (AC 5). They own a footman's pick initially, the symbol of their position in their old tribe.

Special Benefits: Mine rowdies receive a +1 bonus to all die rolls when brawling (punching, wrestling, or overbearing).

Special Hindrances: Because of all the time spent underground, mine rowdies have problems in wide open spaces, such as under an open sky. They suffer a –1 attack penalty when forced to fight in such locations. When not in an underground or enclosed area, they make all proficiency checks at –1.

Wealth Options: Because of their time in mines, mine rowdies start play fairly well off for humanoids, with 4d4 × 10 gp.

Pit Fighter

Pit fighters are humanoids who have been trained to put on a good show for paying customers. In every seedy part of every city, humans and some demihumans frequent hidden battle pits where humanoid pit fighters are matched against each other or some other opponent (probably an animal or captured monster). Betting takes place at these events, but the real entertainment comes from the stunts employed by the pit fighters.

Pit fighters who become player characters have given up the life (if they were slaves) or have decided to supplement their income by adventuring (if they were free pit fighters). Even when fighting alongside adventuring companions, pit fighters battle like they are still in the pits, making fancy moves and playing with their opponents in anticipation of the roar of the crowd.

Requirements: Any humanoid, male or female, except fremlins, can be a pit fighter. Because of their exotic natures and because of the freedom to excel that this kit allows, many female humanoids find their way into the battle pits. There are no special alignment or ability score requirements for this kit.

Role: Like cock fighting, humanoid battle pits are illegal in most human and demihuman cities, towns and villages. However, that does not stop criminals and others seeking monetary gain from engaging in the practice. In large cities and towns, battle pits are hidden in the less-savory areas. In villages, spectators must wait until a traveling show fighting circus makes the circuit to their area. The audience bets on each match, and winners of each match receive a portion of the purse.

Pit fighters can either be slaves or free, using their talents to make money for themselves and their masters. As a slave, the pit fighter fights exclusively for the profit of the owner. In return, the pit fighter receives food and water, weapons, training, and the roar of the crowds. A free pit fighter enters the pits for personal wealth and fame. Free pit fighters usually have an "agent" who assists them in return for a cut of the profits. These agents are normally human or demihuman, so they can more easily act on the pit fighter's behalf in the towns and cities.

Some pit fighters use graceful maneuvers, stunts, and witty banter to put on impressive displays. Such skilled pit fighters are valuable to their masters and rarely forced to fight each other to the death. Instead, they engage in well-choreographed bouts for the entertainment of the audience. When bloodlust takes the crowds, pit fighters are pitted against animals or monsters, where they use their superior skills to methodically and with great fanfare slice their foes to ribbons.

Pit fighters are among the most urban of humanoid character kits. They have an accepted place in human society, and use their spare time to learn whatever they can (if their masters allow it). Even so, they pick up a lot of the local culture just because of their proximity to it. Many pit fighters love to have a good time, often spending the money they earn on gaming, drink, and entertainment.

Many pit fighters take their showy skills adventuring with them. They never battle quietly, rarely go for the quick kill, and often prod their companions to compliment them when no crowds of spectators are present to lavish praise.

Weapon Proficiencies: Members of this kit must have a basic tribal weapon or a short sword proficiency. Other weapon slots should be filled with exotic melee weapons not normally allowed beginning humanoid characters.

Nonweapon Proficiencies:
• Bonus Proficiencies: Close-quarter fighting.
• Recommended, General: Acting (stage fighting), drinking, eating.
• Recommended, Warrior: Endurance, gaming, natural fighting.
• Recommended, Priest: Reading/writing.
• Recommended, Rogue: Crowd working, jumping, tightrope walking, tumbling.
• Forbidden: Hiding, running, wild fighting. These proficiencies can be learned later during

the campaign, should the opportunity arise.

Equipment: A pit fighter is limited to chain mail or lighter armor (AC 5). A shield is also allowed. A pit fighter also starts play with a weapon of specialization (see below).

Special Benefits: Single-classed pit fighters receive a free weapon specialization in any melee weapon.

Any pit fighter is allowed to specialize in more melee weapons after first level by using additional weapon proficiency slots. In addition, any pit fighter can use nonweapon proficiency slots for weapons.

A pit fighter can take rogue proficiencies without spending an extra penalty slot.

Special Hindrances: As pit fighters are trained to make combat last, they receive a –2 penalty to all damage rolls they inflict.

Wealth Options: Though pit fighters can make decent money in the battle pits, they often spend it as fast as they earn it. Each begins play with 3d4 × 10 gp.

Saurial Paladin

Saurial paladins are a rare exception to the inability of nonhumans to become paladins. Saurials come from an alternative setting in which they are the equivalent of humans. While many of the abilities of the saurial paladin are like those of human paladins, the significant differences will be detailed here.

Among humanoid races that are of good alignment, saurial paladins are respected and even revered. Among savage lizard man tribes they may viewed with awe or hostility. The reaction of advanced lizard man tribes will also vary, but to lesser extremes. The evil humanoid races consider saurial paladins with as much malevolence and loathing as they do human paladins.

Requirements: Only finhead saurials can become saurial paladins. Finhead saurials adopting this kit must meet all of the requirements necessary to become paladins, as given in the *Players' Handbook.*

Role: Saurial paladins are respected and honored members of saurial society. They are noble and heroic, the symbol of all that is good and true. While many of these holy warriors remain in saurial territory to help protect it from the evils of the world, a few decide to take the battle to the enemy — crusading to whatever locations where the forces of evil hold sway. Saurial paladins are humble servants of good, quietly doing whatever they have to in their personal war against evil. They are not braggarts or boasters (in fact, they are mute) and few press the tenets of their beliefs upon those who do not want to hear. However, in the presence of true evil, saurial paladins are quick to respond with whatever force is necessary, often taking bold chances and fighting against great odds to achieve their objectives.

Weapon Proficiencies: Saurial paladins are not restricted in weapon use, but a sword proficiency must be taken at first level. See then section on saurials for penalties for the use of non-saurial weapons.

Nonweapon Proficiencies:
• Bonus Proficiencies: None.
• Recommended, General: Direction sense, etiquette, heraldry, riding (land-based).
• Recommended, Warrior: Any except wild fighting.
• Recommended, Priest: Ancient history, healing, reading/writing, religion.
• Forbidden: Wild fighting. This proficiency cannot be taken at any time.

Equipment: Saurial paladins can purchase any type of armor or equipment. They must also acquire the holy symbol of the power they serve before beginning play.

Special Benefits: Saurial paladins have the following special abilities:
• +2 bonus to all saving throws;
• immune to all diseases;
• can "lay on hands" to heal 2 hit points of damage per level per day;
• can *cure disease* once per 5 levels of experience per week;

• can wield *holy swords* with all the benefits available to paladins;

• instead of being able to *detect evil*, they have the innate ability to *know alignment* up to three times per day.

Special Hindrances: Saurial paladins do not radiate *protection from evil*, they cannot turn undead, and they cannot use clerical spells. All of the strictures that apply to paladins apply to saurial paladins, as listed in the *Player's Handbook*. Like all saurials, saurial paladins do not speak.

Wealth Options: Saurial paladins initially receive 4d4 × 5 gp to purchase equipment.

Sellsword

Sellswords are the professional warriors of the humanoid races. They do not fight out of loyalty, or duty, or even to defend their tribe. They fight for money, pure and simple. And the more money involved, the harder they fight. For most of these humanoids, it isn't might that makes right — it's the weight of their employer's purse.

Sellsword player characters lose little of their mercenary tendencies. They still look for monetary compensation for their skills, and some even consider themselves hired warriors attached to an adventuring party, as opposed to a full-share member of the group.

Requirements: All races and either gender (except fremlins) may become sellswords. The character must have a minimum Constitution of 12. A sellsword must have at least a partially neutral alignment.

Role: Humanoid sellswords leave their lairs to fight for others in exchange for money or other compensation. Some may have originally taken up the role to escape former lives, others because their tribes have turned to less violent pursuits and the call of battle still rings in their blood. Now they fight for cash. Many tribes consider sellswords to be traitors to their own kind, for they have decided to use their abili-

ties not in service to the tribe but to fill their own purses.

Some sellswords hire into mercenary forces and are assigned to defend specific areas or wage war in the name of their employers. Others take on more personal jobs as bodyguards, enforcers, or extra muscle. In all cases, sellswords consider themselves as professional soldiers — not as assassins or hired killers.

Sellswords might be hired by villages to clear out marauding monsters, or by towns and cities to guard trade routes, but they are never really accepted in these places. Instead, they are feared, avoided, and relegated to specific areas as part of the terms of their employment. Most people consider humanoid sellswords to be a necessary evil. They may buy their loyalty, but they never trust them completely, keeping one eye on them and one hand on their own swords. Wizards hire sell-swords for a variety of functions, and many evil groups will employ them as low level leaders, thugs, and added muscle.

However, every sellsword has his or her own scruples, with set lines they will not cross no matter how much money is involved. Some will only fight for just causes or against equals, others will not attack innocents, and a few will not battle members of their own race. While some sages claim every sellsword has a price, most of these humanoids in fact display specific compunctions (though they may seem strange and alien to non-humanoid minds).

Player character sellswords may just be coming off a job that turned out well but produced no cash, or one that went terribly and in the end all fees were held back. Maybe they even decided not to finish a job because it went against their own particular code of honor, and are now looking for other work. (Of course, the employer they left high and dry may come after them at some point for recompense.) A humanoid sellsword might join an adventuring party for any number

of reasons, but the bottom line (at least at first) will be "what's in it for the sellsword."

Weapon Proficiencies: All sellswords must start with the short sword or spear, as these weapons are common and easy to acquire even in the worst of times. A third slot is taken up by a character's weapon of choice (from those listed in the race's initial proficiencies). The fourth slot can be any generally available weapon (it is assumed the humanoid has learned to use the weapon in the service of others after leaving its tribe).

Nonweapon Proficiencies:

• Bonus Proficiencies: Survival (same as humanoid's homeland).

• Recommended, General: Animal handling, cooking, fire-building, riding (land-based), weather sense.

• Recommended, Warrior: Bowyer/fletcher, hunting, gaming, looting, running.

• Recommended, Priest: Reading/writing.

• Forbidden: Etiquette, fortune telling, heraldry (other than their own). Sellswords may acquire these proficiencies at a later time.

Equipment: When first starting, sellswords may purchase only one of these armor types: hide, padded, or scale. After their first adventure, they may buy any available armor type.

Special Benefits: Sellswords have the ability to earn money by selling their services. In any situation in which fighters are being hired, the reaction roll of the potential employer is adjusted by +2 in the sellsword's favor. Naturally, employment will not be available all the time, and some jobs will conflict with the current goals of the sellsword's party.

Special Hindrances: Sellswords suffer a reaction penalty of –2 whenever common people encounter them; few trust them and most fear them. Any party with a sellsword as a member has a penalty of –1.

Wealth Options: Sellswords begin with 5d4 × 5 gp. This sum represents what remains of the sellsword's last pay.

Wilderness Protector

Wilderness protectors are the humanoid equivalent of rangers. Some are respected by their tribes and work with them, but most are loners who abhor the selfish and destructive practices of many races and work to counter such excessive behavior.

Player character wilderness protectors join up with adventuring groups in order to accomplish larger goals or to defeat evil monsters they cannot hope to best on their own. When the goals of the group deviate from the wilderness protector's, the humanoid may leave to carry on his own mission.

Requirements: The following humanoid races may select the wilderness protector kit: beastmen, centaurs, voadkyn, minotaurs (rare), saurials, satyrs, and swanmays. Wilderness protectors abide by the requirements listed for the ranger class in the *Player's Handbook*.

Role: Like rangers, wilderness protectors defend the good and watch over forests and woodlands. They are excellent hunters and woodsmen, living by weapons and wits in the great outdoors. They are also ecological crusaders, near-fanatics who have taken it upon themselves to be nature's soldiers in the war they believe is being waged against the land.

Wilderness protectors are preservers of life. They defend nature against obvious threats while seeking out the secretive, more ominous dangers that lie in wait. They consider it their sacred mission to keep the wilderness safe from those who would exploit or destroy it.

Even those races with an affinity toward nature believe wilderness protectors to be fanatics. Most also consider them to be touched by the gods, and while they will have little to do with the protectors, they will not hinder them in any way.

Wilderness protectors are normally solitary beings, though they will team up with others in order to carry on their crusade. To many, the protectors seem crazed and quick to violence,

but they never raise sword except in defense of life and nature. However, any slight against nature receives the same response. They love life and all its pleasures, living wild and free in the wilderness.

Player character protectors will join adventuring groups for a time, but they always keep their personal crusade foremost in their minds. They always try to persuade the group to help them, often while admonishing or lecturing them on their environmentally harmful habits. If the mission of the group ever contradicts or totally ignores the mission of the protector, he or she will depart. If the group ever performs deeds that are directly opposed to the protector's mission, the protector may be forced to confront them.

Weapon Proficiencies: Any.

Nonweapon Proficiencies:

• Bonus Proficiencies: Survival (woodlands), tracking.

• Recommended, General: Animal handling, animal noise, animal training, direction sense, hiding, leatherworking, riding (land based), swimming, weather sense.

• Recommended, Warrior: Animal lore, bowyer/fletcher, fishing, hunting, natural fighting, set snares, wild fighting.

• Recommended, Priest: Healing, herbalism, local history, religion, spellcraft.

• Recommended, Wizard: None.

• Recommended, Rogue: None.

• Forbidden: Charioteering, seamanship.

Equipment: Wilderness protectors cannot wear any armor heavier than studded leather. They cannot retain more equipment or treasure than they can carry.

Special Benefits: Wilderness protectors have all the special abilities of rangers as defined in the *Player's Handbook*.

Special Hindrances: Wilderness protectors have all of the limitations of rangers as defined in the *Player's Handbook*. In addition, they suffer a 3-point penalty to initial reactions of NPCs encountered.

Wealth Options: Wilderness protectors start out poor. Each begins with 3d4 × 5 gp.

Wizard Kits

Perhaps the least encountered humanoid is the wizard humanoid. Magic and spellcraft are not easily learned, and few humanoid races maintain formal magical instruction. For one thing, literacy is not a distinguishing feature of many of the less advanced humanoid cultures. All humanoid wizards must have the reading/writing proficiency. If their native language does not have a written form, then they must know a language that does.

These kits represent the rare humanoid individuals who leave their homes behind because the call of magic flows inside them. These individuals have sought out magical knowledge and training wherever they could find it, and have learned enough to enter the wizard class. Note that humanoids cannot become specialist wizards (it is difficult enough for them to become generalists!). Here is an overview of the humanoid wizard kits:

• *Hedge wizards* usually dwell alone, if not apart from the tribal community, with perhaps an apprentice for company. They rely on their reputations to keep away the unwanted as they pursue their researches. They have some facility with potions, and a brisk trade of charms, trinkets, and elixirs going on the side.

• *Humanoid scholars* leave their tribes to learn more about the world at large — and about magic in particular. Through their travels and studies, they have become wizards. Their quest for knowledge and love of ancient history keeps them forever on the move.

• *Outlaw mages* use the magic they have learned to eke out a living through thievery and robbery. These humanoids combine thief skills with magic to steal from the rich and give — to themselves (in most cases), though some share the spoils with the oppressed in their areas.

Hedge Wizard

Hedge wizards are humanoids who have learned magic through private study. Though they are usually hermits or social outcasts, they will often provide aid in time of need, though they realize that no hedge wizards are really trusted by those around them. They are often blamed for general misfortune: bad weather, poor crops, soured milk, bad luck.

Hedge wizards spend their time puttering about, collecting unusual objects for study, searching for odd and obscure facts, recording keen observations, and carrying on mysterious researches that keep the humanoids around them in awe and fear. They sometimes disappear for weeks at a time, only to suddenly reappear with unique counsel, a singular item, or an experimental solution to a local problem.

Requirements: This kit can be taken by any humanoid wizard, regardless of race, gender, or alignment. This kit requires a minimum Intelligence of 9.

Role: While most other humanoids tend to leave hedge wizards alone, there is always a small traffic in charms, tonics, elixirs, love potions, and the like, which the hedge wizard provides. Hedge wizards will often work with adventurers or most skillful hunters in the community, for they always require odd components and rare commodities for their researches. In return, the hedge wizard provides knowledge, advice, and the odd potion.

Hedge wizards often take on apprentices to keep up their dwelling places and assist with their observations and experiments. The most adept apprentices may eventually become hedge wizards themselves.

Fremlins taking this kit are usually more interested in having the reputation than in actually doing any real work. They also tend to develop obscure and fairly useless proficiencies, such as Blowing Smoke Rings.

Weapon Proficiencies: Hedge wizards can use any weapon allowed to standard wizards.

Nonweapon Proficiencies:
• Bonus Proficiencies: Herbalism.
• Required Proficiencies: Reading/writing.
• Recommended, General: Agriculture (gardening), cooking, fire-building, fortune-telling, observation.
• Recommended, Warrior: None.
• Recommended, Priest: Healing.
• Recommended, Wizard: Languages (ancient), local history, spellcraft.
• Recommended, Rogue: Disguise.

Equipment: Hedge wizards can have any equipment used by standard mages, if it is available in the hedge wizard's locale.

Special Benefits: A hedge wizard can *create antidote* for any poison. Brewing takes up to a day (assuming materials are available). The brew remains effective for three days per level of the wizard. Its chance of successfully countering a poison is 25% + 5% per wizard's level.

At 7th level, the hedge wizard can brew magical potions. The formula for each type of potion must be researched separately, according to the guidelines in the *Dungeon Master's Guide*. To make the potion, the hedge wizard must collect the proper ingredients.

Special Hindrances: Hedge wizards are restricted to the following schools of magic: abjuration, conjuration, divination, and enchantment/charm. They can also take *either* illusion/phantasm or necromancy. They cannot learn spells from forbidden schools.

Wealth Options: Hedge wizards start with (1d4 + 1) × 10 gp.

Humanoid Scholar

Humanoid scholars travel the world to study and learn everything they can about a given subject — always magic, though some humanoids have additional areas of scholarly interest. This has given them spellcasting skills, which they use to continue their studies. While humanoid scholars do not have to be at odds with their tribes, the nature of their lifestyle takes them out into the world at large.

Requirements: This kit is available to the following humanoid races: centaurs, fremlins, minotaurs, mongrelmen, ogre magi, and saurials. It is open to all genders and alignments, but the scholar must have an Wisdom of 11 or better.

Role: Humanoid scholars love to search through ruins, dungeons, and dusty libraries. They spend large amounts of time examining books, scrolls and other writings in order to add to the wealth of knowledge already filling their heads. While humanoid scholars may eventually become good teachers, they spend their early years too busy gathering information to pass along what they have learned.

Humanoid scholars are rare among their own kind, for few humanoids have the patience or desire to learn more than they need to know to survive. Members of this kit are motivated to learn more and more about the world, specific subjects, and magic in general. They practice what they learn of spellcraft by becoming magic-users of no small skill.

Some humanoid scholars even decide to become historians, recording the chronicles of their own lives and the lives of the adventurers

they work with. In fact, some of these humanoids will join an adventuring party just so they can write down the events which occur around them. Others become adventurers to seek out old books and dusty scrolls, to explore lost sites, and to meet with ancient beings and forgotten cultures who can add to their store of knowledge.

Humanoid scholars are usually not violent, and few show many passions that are not related to their pursuit of knowledge and magic. Most are seen as unopposing and quiet — at least until the first artifact or ancient tome is uncovered. Then they become animated, taking charge of the situation so that the knowledge in question falls into their care.

Weapon Proficiencies: Any weapon normally available to wizards.

Nonweapon Proficiencies:

• Bonus Proficiencies: Reading/writing (common), two other (see benefits).

• Required Proficiencies: Ancient history or local history.

• Recommended, General: Heraldry, language (modern), looting (knowledge only), poetry, reading/writing.

• Recommended, Warrior: None.

• Recommended, Priest: None.

• Recommended, Wizard: Ancient history, languages (ancient), local history, religion, spellcraft.

• Recommended, Rogue: None.

• Forbidden: Blind-fighting, close-quarter fighting, running, wild fighting.

Equipment: Humanoid scholars use any weapons normally available to wizards.

Special Benefits: Humanoid scholars receive two free nonweapon proficiencies. These must be chosen from the recommended proficiencies.

Special Hindrances: Except for one proficiency, all of the scholar's initial proficiencies must be spent on skills relating to the pursuit of knowledge.

Wealth Options: Humanoid scholars start play with (1d4 + 1) x 10 gp.

Outlaw Mage

The outlaw mage is a humanoid who has learned magic and uses it to profit outside the law, or at least outside the grasp of the local ruling authority. By combining a humanoid's natural thieving tendencies with wizard spells, an outlaw mage can survive and become rich through illusion, deception, and spellcraft. Outlaw mages usually engage in one specific rogue-like activity, either banditry or burglary. They supplement their physical and stealth abilities with spellcasting to waylay travelers or break into guarded locations.

Requirements: This kit is only available to the following humanoid races: centaurs, fremlins, voadkyn, minotaurs, mongrelmen, ogre magi, and saurials. Outlaw mages can be either gender, but they must select a non-good alignment. Members of this kit must have a minimum Dexterity score of 9.

Role: Outlaw mages rarely operate within the structure of humanoid tribes. They are loners who have left the tribe to follow the call of magic. To supplement their studies, they learned to rob and steal, and now employ both magic and rogue-like tricks to survive. Though they are loners, outlaw mages frequently operate with others. Like witch doctors, outlaw mages often advise the leaders of outlaw gangs —and sometimes they even take charge of such gangs, leaving the advising to others.

These humanoids are often found in service to evil wizards and others who walk the darker paths of society. They sometimes indenture themselves to such personages in order to learn more magic. While not all outlaw mages are specifically evil, all operate outside the laws of the land — be it human, demihuman, or humanoid law.

Outlaw mages who join player characters have not given up a life of crime, they have just decided to throw in with adventurers in order to put their talents to more structured use. Every group of adventurers requires the ser-

vices of thieves and wizards. The outlaw mage provides both sets of skills in the form of a single humanoid character.

Some outlaw mages steal from the rich to give to the poor (at least a little), while others engage in robbery to fill their own pockets. No outlaw mages like to fight, and they are at a decided disadvantage in physical confrontations. If they cannot win through magic, thievery or wits, they usually make a strategic retreat. There will always be another traveler to rob or a keep to break into, so better to run, hide, and wait for a better day than to try to fight a stronger opponent.

Weapon Proficiencies: Outlaw mages can take any weapon available to wizards.

Nonweapon Proficiencies:
• Bonus Proficiencies: Hiding.
• Required Proficiencies: reading/writing (common).
• Recommended, General: Acting, begging, danger sense, fast-talking, looting, riding (land based).
• Recommended, Warrior: None.
• Recommended, Priest: None.
• Recommended, Wizard: Languages (modern), reading/writing, spellcraft.
• Recommended, Rogue: Appraising, disguise, gaming, reading lips, tightrope walking, ventriloquism.
• Forbidden: Blind-fighting, close-quarter fighting, natural fighting, wild fighting. Outlaw mages can never learn these proficiencies.

Equipment: Outlaw mages may use any weapons or equipment available to wizards.

Special Benefits: Outlaw mages may take rogue proficiencies without spending an extra slot. Also, the outlaw mage can take thieves' cant as a language selection.

Special Hindrances: None.

Wealth Options: Outlaw mages receive (1d4 + 1) × 10 gp initially.

Priest Kits

Humanoids follow a vast number of gods. Some are powerful, some are not, but all grant spells to their followers. Most humanoid holy men and women are shamans, though clerics and specialist priests are available to many races. Remember, if a humanoid becomes a player character, he or she may have to abandon the gods of his or her race. This is especially true in the case of truly evil deities. Humanoids who normally would worship a deity that is diametrically opposed to their player character alignment must select a god more in line with his new beliefs.

A DM using the *Monster Mythology* and/or *Legends & Lore* rules supplements may allow humanoids to become specialty priests, as described in the *Player's Handbook*.

Here is an overview of the humanoid priest kits:

• *Shamans* are humanoids who use their divinely given powers to help their community. They are more concerned with their flock than with their faith. Most priests in primitive tribes will be shamans. Druids and shamans will not be found in the same tribe.

• *Witch doctors* are humanoids who combine priestly abilities with limited magic use. They are a variation of shaman, and the two will seldom be found in the same humanoid tribe.

• *Oracles* always look to the future, using their skills and powers to interpret omens and signs. They are the keepers of the superstitions, the priests of fear and folklore.

• *War priests* are humanoids who combine cleric magic with fighting skills. They administer to the more violent, warlike tribes, often wading into battle besides the tribe's soldiers. War priests are truly warriors of their faiths.

• *Wandering mystics* leave their tribes to preach the tenets of their faith to others. Characters who have rejected their racial gods often become wandering mystics dedicated to a god not often worshipped by others of their kind.

Shaman

As the primitive equivalent of priests in their primitive cultures, shamans are the mediators between the powers and spirits outside the tribe and the tribe members. They are not as formal or regimented as other priests, and have a far more practical, down-to-earth manner. While priests are most often identified the god they follow, shamans are most often identified with their tribe.

Requirements: The shaman kit is only available to the following humanoid races: Aarakocras, alaghi, bugbears, bullywugs, centaurs, firbolgs, voadkyn, gnolls, flinds, goblins, hobgoblins, kobolds, lizard men, mongrelmen, ogres, half-ogres, ogre mages, orcs, half-orcs, and wemics. Shaman gender is restricted only by tribal custom, and they can be of any alignment which matches their tribe or god.

Role: The well-being of the community is the most important thing to the shaman, for they are the repository of the lore and wisdom of the tribe. No problem is too trivial for a shaman to care about. They provide divinations, though the form is often improvised and the source of information is usually dubious. They give sympathy and moral support, healing ills with skills and folk remedies more often than with spells, and teach the young what they will need to serve the community.

Shamans must undergo arduous rituals before taking their posts, as well as serving as an apprentice to the previous shaman. These include long periods of fasting, initiation ceremonies that require some amount of pain and suffering, and even trials of danger.

Most adventuring PC shamans have a greater purpose. Some adventure to aid their tribe. Others adventure as part of their initiation, and have a specific quest goal that must be met before they can return to their tribe. Still others are the last survivors of their tribes. Guilt-ridden because they failed to protect their tribes from whatever destroyed them, they now consider their adven-turing party to be their new tribe. The rarest shaman PC is one who has rejected the ways of his race. These shamans seek to perform their duties, possibly to a new tribe. Until they can find a tribe that needs them and that has similar beliefs, these shamans will minister to an adventuring party.

Weapon Proficiencies: Shamans have access to the weapons available to standard priests, and they can also choose tribal weapons.

Nonweapon Proficiencies:
• Bonus Proficiencies: Local history.
• Recommended, General: Agriculture, animal training, fire-building, fishing, fortune telling, rope use, weather sense, weaving, winemaking.
• Recommended, Warrior: Animal lore, mountaineering, set snares.
• Recommended, Priest: Healing, herbalism, religion, spellcraft.
• Recommended, Wizard: None.
• Recommended, Rogue: None.
• Forbidden: Etiquette, heraldry, reading/writing. These proficiencies may be learned during the course of a campaign.

Equipment: Shamans use weapons and armor typical for their tribe and the powers served. They can use any clerical magical items, save scrolls.

Special Benefits: Shamans can learn the healing and herbalism proficiencies at the cost of one proficiency slot each.

At 9th level, shamans can cast the *reincarnation* spell as a 5th level spell.

Magical Abilities: Shamans may only choose spells from up to three different spheres from the list given for specialty priests. These spheres will never change.

Special Hindrances: Shamans use six-sided dice (d6) when determining their hit points, not eight-sided dice as other clerics.

Shamans cannot turn or control undead.

Shamans never receive direct access to the *raise dead* or *resurrection* spells.

Wealth Options: Shamans begin play with 3d6 × 5 gp.

Witch Doctor

Witch doctors are a somewhat rarer version of shamans, combining shamanism with magical ability. Much of the background and role of the witch doctor is identical to that of the shaman, and all shaman abilities, benefits, and restrictions apply to the witch doctor as well. Generally a tribe will have shamans or witch doctors, not both.

Requirements: The witch doctor kit is only available to the following humanoid races: bugbears, gnolls, flinds, goblins, hobgoblins, kobolds, minotaurs, half-ogres, orcs, half-orcs, and wemics. Witch doctor gender is restricted only by tribal custom, and they can be of any alignment. Witch doctors must have a minimum Intelligence of 9.

Role: Witch doctors walk within the twilight between wizardry and priestly magic. On one hand, they function as shamans for their tribe. At the same time, they make use of wizard spells, employing magic to defend the tribe and establish their own power.

Because humanoids are impressed, awed, and made fearful by magic, witch doctors hold positions of great influence in their tribes. They often act as advisors to the chiefs, giving counseling and support to their leaders.

Most primitive humanoids are very superstitious, and sometimes turn against the witch doctor. A witch doctor who cannot regain his authority must flee or be killed. (This might be the background for a PC witch doctor.)

If a master witch doctor has more than one apprentice, only one will receive the mantle of tribal witch doctor when the master retires or dies. The others are banished or killed to keep the harmony of the tribe intact. Other apprentices leave when there is no more that the master can teach them.

Weapon Proficiencies: Witch doctors have access to the weapons available to wizards, and they can also choose tribal weapons.

Nonweapon Proficiencies:
• Bonus Proficiencies: Local history.
• Recommended, General: Agriculture, crowd working, dancing, singing, winemaking.
• Recommended, Warrior: None.
• Recommended, Priest: Healing, religion.
• Recommended, Wizard: Astrology, herbalism, languages (ancient), spellcraft.
• Recommended, Rogue: None.
• Forbidden: Heraldry.

Equipment: Witch doctors can use any weapon with which they can become proficient. They cannot wear armor of any type. They can use any magical items normally usable by wizards.

Special Benefits: Witch doctors have all the special benefits of shamans.

Witch doctors can take wizard proficiencies without spending an extra slot.

Special Hindrances: Witch doctors are limited to a single school of magic (though they have none of the bonuses or penalties of specialist wizards).

Witch doctors cast wizard spells like wizards of one-half their level (round up). Thus, a 5th level witch doctor can cast wizard spells as a 3rd level wizard.

A witch doctor cannot gain priest or wizard spells outside the chosen spheres and school.

Wealth Options: Witch doctors begin play with (1d4 + 1) × 5 gp.

Oracle

Oracles are humanoid clerics or druids who believe themselves to be the mouthpieces of the gods. They foretell the future, interpret signs and omens, and speak to their people with the authority of the gods. Oracles often follow a pantheon as opposed to a single deity, bringing the words of all to the ears of the tribes. They are the keepers of folklore and mystery, the clerics of fear and superstition. They tend to be isolated even when they are part of a community.

Oracle player characters usually join adventuring parties as part of a grand quest for their deities or to bring the words of their gods to others who could profit by them.

Requirements: This kit is available to the following humanoid races: alaghi, bugbears, centaurs, gnolls, flinds, goblins, hobgoblins, kobolds, mongrelmen, half-ogres, orcs, half-orcs, saurials, and swanmays. Oracles can be male or female. Their alignment must match that of their deity or the pantheon they follow. There are no special ability score requirements.

Role: Oracles deliver broad statements about the future to followers of their faith (or to anyone else to whom they feel compelled to preach). These humanoids believe that they are receiving visions from their gods, and they help other followers to act on them accordingly. They provide guidance, they interpret omens, and they often assist those they are compelled to present prophecy to. When they go on these vision quests, they may just watch to see how the prophecy comes to pass, or they may help it to unfold.

As humanoids are extremely superstitious, these clerics take it upon themselves to administer to their fears and superstitious practices. For this reason, oracles are sometimes called "priests of fear." While it may appear to outsiders that they are just taking advantage of the superstitious tendencies of humanoid tribes, oracles actually serve a legitimate purpose. They counsel humanoids on how best to work through their fears, teaching them to lead productive lives despite the many superstitions that hang over them.

Of course, they believe that superstitions are real — to ignore them is to invite disaster and the wrath of the spirit world. At times when a superstition completely hampers a humanoid, the oracle reads the signs and omens in order to find a way to appease the spirits and break the paralyzing fear.

Oracle player characters always speak of visions and the future. They will allow nothing to be done until they read the signs and por-

tents. While this could get on the nerves of less-superstitious party members, oracles also bring with them a number of skills and abilities which make them very good companions to have around. In addition, these characters can also serve as tools of the DM through which valuable clues (and red herrings) can be passed along.

Weapon Proficiencies: Oracles must select their weapons from those allowed to priests.

Nonweapon Proficiencies:

• Bonus Proficiencies: Danger sense.

• Recommended, General: Chanting, direction sense, observation, weather sense.

• Recommended, Warrior: Survival.

• Recommended, Priest: Astrology, reading/writing, religion, spellcraft.

• Recommended, Wizard: None.

• Recommended, Rogue: Information gathering, ventriloquism.

• Forbidden: None.

Equipment: Oracles may use any armor and equipment allowed to their class.

Special Benefits: Oracles have the ability to *receive visions* of the future twice per month. These visions will be true, although they may be highly symbolic and open to many interpretations. Other visions may come unbidden, but these may or may not be true.

Magical Abilities: Druidic oracles have access to the standard druidic spheres. Other oracles have following spells.

• Major Access: All, Divination, Protection, Sun.

• Minor Access: Charm, Guardian, Healing, and Necromantic.

• Forbidden Spheres: All others.

Oracles can turn or control undead as other clerics.

Special Hindrances: Oracles will receive no clear visions regarding events in which they are fated to play an active role. Using a vision for personal gain immediately draws a *curse* (in the form of a penalty imposed by the DM).

Wealth Options: Oracles receive 3d6 × 5 gp initially.

War Priest

War priests are clerics of battle. These humanoids preach a doctrine of might as right, administering to the body as much as to the soul. Not only do they bring the faith to the warrior classes, they also fight beside them when they march to war. War priests are clerics with better than average combat skills. They burn with the indignation of their violent gods, wielding weapon and holy symbol in harmony for the faith they believe.

When war priests become player characters, they may turn away from the evil deities of their tribes, but they quickly find new gods to replace them. These gods may be less evil, but they are no less violent. These priests follow war gods and only war gods.

Requirements: This kit is only available to the following humanoid races: bugbears, gnolls, flinds, goblins, hobgoblins, kobolds, half-ogres, orc, half-orcs, and saurials. War priests can be male or female, and they can be of any alignment. The minimum Strength score required for members of this kit is 12.

Role: War priests lead the faithful to battle, bringing cleric spells to the battlefield along with their weapons of choice. They are respected among those races which engage in war as a way of life, and feared among those races that prefer more peaceful solutions.

War priests usually attend to the spiritual needs of warriors, considering others as less worthy of their attention. They foretell when the gods want their followers to go to war. They prepare the troops with inspirational sermons and clerical blessings. They fight alongside their followers, bringing the wrath of their gods upon their enemies.

War priests often become adventurers at the bequest of their deity. They often go on long quests as part of their normal duties. Others turn away from their gods to take up the other faiths. To prove their loyalty to their new gods, these war priests may also take up holy quests at the side of adventuring parties.

Weapon Proficiencies: War priests wield the weapon of their war god.

Nonweapon Proficiencies:
- Bonus Proficiencies: Wild fighting.
- Required Proficiencies: Religion.
- Recommended, General: Endurance, intimidation, riding (land based).
- Recommended, Warrior: Armorer, blacksmithing, blind-fighting, close-quarter fighting, weaponsmithing.
- Recommended, Priest: Engineering, healing, spellcraft.
- Recommended, Wizard: None.
- Recommended, Rogue: None.
- Forbidden: None.

Equipment: War priests may purchase any equipment they choose, including any armor and any weapons. They can use any magical items normally available to priests.

Special Benefits: War priests can acquire warrior proficiencies without spending an extra slot.

Magical Abilities: War priests are allowed the following spells.
- Major Access: All, Combat, Healing, Protection.
- Minor Access: Guardian, Necromantic, Divination, Sun.
- Forbidden Spheres: All others.

War priests can turn or control undead as other priests.

Special Hindrances: None.

Wealth Options: War priests start play with 3d6 × 5 gp.

Wandering Mystic

Wandering mystics are humanoid clerics who leave their tribes to preach to others. They either go in search of converts to their race's faith, or, if they have rejected their race's deities, they seek to bring the tenets of a new religion to those who have not yet heard them.

Player character wandering mystics join up with adventuring parties to serve as their spiri-

tual guides or to accomplish some great task for their gods. No matter what mission the party may be involved with, a wandering mystic will take every opportunity to find converts to his or her faith.

Requirements: This kit is available to the following humanoid races: alaghi, bugbears, centaurs, gnolls, flinds, goblins, hobgoblins, kobolds, mongrelmen, half-ogres, orcs, half-orcs, saurials, and swanmays. This kit is open to all genders and alignments.

Role: Wandering mystics come in two forms. The first is a cleric of a particular humanoid race who receives a vision to preach to those beyond the limits of the tribe's territory. The second is a cleric who finds faith not in the gods of his race but in a totally foreign deity. While this cleric may try to convert his own tribe, he will quickly decide to find converts in less-hostile locations.

Wandering mystics are voices in the wilderness, attached to no organized temple or religion. They are loners on missions for the gods they serve, traveling wherever their faith leads them. A wandering mystic can be a strange sight, striding out of the wilderness with

words of inspiration for all who would hear. While they might sometimes work with those clerics of their gods who are attached to an organized religion, more often than not they are at odds with these clerics. They do not believe in the trappings of tradition and regiment. They preach a looser, less confining form of spiritual worship.

Player character wandering mystics may appear disheveled, distant, and even crazed. They follow voices only they can hear and see sights meant for no other eyes. When they join with an adventuring party, it is because they are following the will of their gods.

Weapon Proficiencies: Any weapon normally available to mystic's base priest class can be selected by the mystic.

Nonweapon Proficiencies:
• Bonus Proficiencies: Survival (of choice).
• Required Proficiencies: Fire-building.
• Recommended, General: Agriculture, animal handling, carpentry, cobbling, cooking, fishing, leatherworking, pottery, seamstress/tailor, stonemasonry, weaving.
• Recommended, Warrior: Endurance, survival.
• Recommended, Priest: Healing, herbalism, local history.
• Recommended, Wizard: None.
• Recommended, Rogue: None.
• Forbidden: None.

Equipment: Wandering mystics may use any weapon or armor available to their base priest class.

Special Benefits: None.

Magical Abilities: Wandering mystics have the sphere selection of their base priest class. They turn undead like their base class.

Special Hindrances: Wandering mystics start play poor (see Wealth Options).

Wandering mystics suffer a 2-point penalty to reaction rolls when dealing with religious NPCs (of any faith, including their own).

Wealth Options: Wandering mystics start with one weapon and 3d6 gp.

Rogue Kits

The second most common occupation for humanoids to take up is rogue, and most races excel as thieves of all kinds. Many humanoids are not equipped for the rigors of the warrior lifestyle, and fewer still have what it takes to advance as priests or wizards. But most share traits that make them prime candidates for rogue professions — greed, caution, skulking, and a love of the dark. Here is an overview of the humanoid rogue kits:

• *Scavengers* search the wilderness for wealth and treasure, living off the discarded goods of others. They are crafty, shrewd, and able to spot a jewel in a mound of garbage. Many make good traders, coming to the cities to offer their finds to those with gold to spare. Of course, not everything they sell is as it appears to be.

• *Tramps* are humanoids who frequent towns and cities, earning a living by begging and engaging in minor thievery. They are excellent pick-pockets and informants, sweeping through crowds in search of wealth and information to sell.

• *Tunnel rats* are humanoids trained to explore underground passages for their tribes. They are experts at underground survival and locating and disarming traps. Other humanoids call them "bait," for they are cast out into the tunnels to see what bites.

• *Shadows* are humanoids who hire themselves out as eliminators. They are humanoid assassins, feared and respected for their deadly skills. Most assassin guilds have at least one shadow among their membership, for there are times when their particular talents are called for.

• *Humanoid bards* are just that, humanoids with the skills and abilities of bards. While this is the closest many humanoids can get to this character class, there are certain differences that separate them from their human and demihuman counterparts.

Scavenger

Scavengers combine a number of skills and abilities to create a unique humanoid character kit. They are expert hunters and searchers, able to locate salvageable items in all types of wilderness terrain. They are artists and craftsmen, able to fix up what they find (at least as far as surface details are concerned) to sell it at a profit. They are cunning and shrewd, crafty peddlers and traders who can usually get the best price for their wares — and perhaps a good bit more.

Player character scavengers have never lost their desire to poke around garbage and other discarded goods. Nothing thrills a humanoid scavenger more than to discover a bright treasure beneath a mound of junk. Often, an adventuring scavenger takes up with other adventurers to secure protection as the hunt for salvageable wares continues.

Requirements: None. Any humanoid rogue, regardless of race, can be a scavenger. Scavengers can be of any alignment or gender.

Role: Scavengers fill a role similar to that of their animal counterparts — they live off the remains of others. These remains can be figurative or literal, for scavengers look for salvageable goods among discarded waste and on the bodies of the dead.

Scavengers rarely operate as members of a humanoid tribe. More often, they are outcasts who turn to picking through the garbage of others to survive. Some even team up with other outcasts to create scavenger gangs, but this is rare. Most scavengers prefer to keep whatever treasures they find for themselves.

Scavengers often look like garbage pickers — they are dirty, dusty, grimy, and often have an unpleasant stench about them. Those just back from a scavenger hunt might also be surrounded by flies and other insects, though most other scavengers would hardly notice. Even when a scavenger tries to make himself presentable before approaching a village to hawk his wares, the telltale signs of dirt and stench linger gently about him, marking the scavenger for what he is.

While a scavenger will be proficient with the normal thieving skills, these are rarely used except in the pursuit of salvage. These humanoids do not believe in stealing as such (except when haggling for trade, see below), for they see garbage and the dead as prime treasure to be sought and salvaged. It is not stealing to take what has been discarded, lost, or forgotten. In fact, scavengers will often follow war parties to pick at the remains of battle the way vultures pick at bones.

For all his disheveled appearance, the scavenger is a shrewd tradesman. He repairs and cleans up the treasures he finds, turning worthless junk into desirable wares. When enough items have accumulated, it's time to go to a village or town to peddle the wares. Few can get the better of a scavenger in a trade — this is usually where they make most of their wealth. While they will sell items of true worth (if they do not want to keep them), more often scavengers sell junk disguised as treasure. They can clean and repair weapons and armor to make them look like new, but the first real use of these items will reveal them as well-polished garbage that breaks under the least bit of pressure.

Weapon Proficiencies: Members of this kit may select any weapons and equipment normally available to thieves.

Nonweapon Proficiencies:
• Bonus Proficiencies: Looting.
• Required proficiencies: Appraising.
• Recommended, General: Artistic ability, blacksmithing, carpentry, direction sense, fast-talking, leatherworking, pottery, riding (land based), seamstress/tailor, weaving.
• Recommended, Warrior: Survival (as appropriate), tracking, weaponsmithing.
• Recommended, Priest: None.
• Recommended, Wizard: None.
• Recommended, Rogue: Ancient history, forgery, gem cutting, local history.
• Forbidden: Reading/writing. Scavengers

know the value of books and scrolls, but lack the ability to read or write. They can learn this proficiency during the course of a campaign.

Equipment: Scavengers can purchase and use any equipment and armor usable by thieves. In addition, they must spend one-quarter of their starting funds on trade wares. The money represents all that was involved to turn salvaged items into trade goods.

Special Benefits: When meeting others in order to peddle salvaged wares, a scavenger receives a +2 reaction bonus.

Special Hindrances: In all other situations, a scavenger's appearance (and stench) grants him a –2 reaction penalty.

Wealth Options: Scavengers begin play with 2d6 × 5 gp.

Tramp

While scavengers pick through the garbage of the wilderness, tramps search the waste of civilization. These humanoids are beggars and thieves, asking for donations with one hand and stealing a heavy purse with the other. In many ways, tramps resemble scavengers — they wear rags and ripped, dirty clothing, they smell bad, and they often seem sickly or crazed. But tramps live among humans and demihumans, surviving on generous donations either freely given or secretly taken.

Tramp player characters often join adventuring parties for a change of pace. While the streets and alleys have excitements all their own, tramps sometimes yearn for true adventures. Of course, they must convince the party that they have skills to offer that will make their inclusion worthwhile.

Requirements: Any humanoid rogue can take the tramp kit.

Role: Tramps are humanoid outcasts who wind up in human towns and cities. For a variety of reasons, they have left their tribes and come to the cities to find their fortunes. Unfortunately, humanoids are not always welcome,

and honest jobs are hard to find. At first, these characters turn to begging in order to earn a living, and they quickly become very good at it. But as time passes, they discover that they must sometimes turn to other means to survive. At these times, tramps learn to take what they require. They consider the coins and items they steal to be alms which are rightfully theirs — it's just that the good people forgot to drop these items in their begging bowls.

Tramps often set up on a busy street, begging for coins from passersby. Tramps may appear sickly and in need of alms, but they are perfectly able-bodied. To them, begging is a career and an art, as honorable as any other profession. Using disguise and acting skills, a tramp will have one particular identity on one corner, and a completely different identity on another. They use a variety of pity-inducing ploys, fast-talking, and sad stories to earn the charity of strangers.

These humanoids have excellent observation skills, and many sell information to those who seek it. Tramps know when new people arrive in their part of the city, they notice any unusual activity going on, and they quickly spot easy marks — those who will give generously of their own accord, or with a little help from the tramp. They are always listening for gossip and rumors, and they know when important, well-paying members of society are looking for particular bits of information.

When information gathering and begging fail to produce enough revenue, tramps wander the crowds in search of pockets to pick and purses to cut. Some even engage in such activity for the fun, excitement and challenge it provides, for street begging can become dreadfully boring after a time. Tramps will not take unnecessary risks, preferring challenges that are well within the scope of their abilities. They even turn to shoplifting when a particularly tempting item catches their eyes.

As player characters, tramps provide a variety of skills to an adventuring party. They are masters of disguise, decent spies, consummate

actors, and professional thieves. They are also cowardly, unsavory, and greedy to a fault, but nobody's perfect.

Weapon Proficiencies: Tramps choose their two initial weapons from the following selection: club, dagger, dart, knife, sling, and staff.
Nonweapon Proficiencies:
  • Bonus Proficiencies: Begging.
  • Required Proficiencies: Observation.
  • Recommended, General: Acting, alertness, fast-talking, fortune telling, hiding, voice mimicry.
  • Recommended, Warrior: Survival (urban).
  • Recommended, Priest: None.
  • Recommended, Wizard: None.
  • Recommended, Rogue: Appraising, disguise, forgery, gaming, information gathering, juggling, local history, reading lips.
  • Forbidden: None.

Equipment: Tramps have very little in the way of equipment. They cannot afford to appear even marginally well off. At most, they carry a simple bowl and a weapon that can be hidden beneath their beat-up clothing. When not engaged in begging or other low-profile activities, tramps can wear any armor and carry any weapons usable by thieves.

Special Benefits: Tramps are particularly adept at sizing up potential targets. By making a successful observation proficiency check, a tramp can accurately determine the subject's class group. A second check can be made to determine the character's level. If this check succeeds, the tramp learns whether the level of the subject is less than his own (yes or no). A roll of 1 on either check reveals exact information. If the subject is disguised, a –5 penalty applies to both types of check.

Special Hindrances: Tramps suffer a –3 reaction roll penalty when dealing with characters who aren't thieves.

For every point of visible AC better than their natural armor class, tramps suffer a –1 penalty to their begging proficiency checks.

Wealth Options: Tramps begin play very little money, receiving only 2d6 gp.

Tunnel Rat

Tunnel rats come from the ranks of all humanoid races that dwell beneath the earth. They serve as advance scouts and explorers for their tribes, using whatever skills they can pick up to survive the unknown dangers waiting below the ground. The good ones have learned to be keen observers and decent fighters, for they must be able to spot natural and artificial traps before they stumble into them, and they must be able to defend themselves against other subterranean races and the monsters that dwell below. The bad ones are all dead.

Player character tunnel rats perform the same services for adventuring parties as they did for their tribes. They take the point, using their skills and abilities to pick a safe path through dungeons and underground tunnels. When they encounter dangers, they warn their companions and take the necessary steps to make the way safe.

Requirements: Tunnel rats must come from the races that live and labor beneath the ground. Of those humanoids detailed in this book, the following may select this kit: goblins, hobgoblins, kobolds, orcs, and half-orcs. There are no special alignment or gender requirements. A tunnel rat usually has a lower Strength or Constitution than is typical.

Role: Tunnel rats serve as bait for the humanoid tribes which live and work in subterranean areas. At least that's how their fellows view them. When humanoids find new tunnels to explore and new mines to dig, or when they decide to spy on their underground neighbors, the first thing they do is select a member of the tribe to be "bait." Ropes are attached to the bait and it is sent into the unexplored tunnel to search for traps, hostile creatures, and other dangers. If the rope reaches the end of its length and nothing bad happens, then the rest of the tribe knows it's relatively safe to follow the bait into the tunnel. Those that survive this particular job often become quite skilled.

When this occurs, they are no longer called bait. They earn the title of tunnel rat.

Even successful tunnel rats rarely achieve high regard in the tribe. They are the butt of jokes, seen as poor fighters because they do not get to fight with the rest of the warriors. They are also considered extremely expendable, for their job is to find dangers before the rest of the tribe can be hurt. As finding these dangers often means death, all tunnel rats are considered to be living on borrowed time. If a tunnel rat dies by stumbling into a trap, causing a cave-in, or springing an ambush, then he has done his job. There are no tears, for more bait is waiting to be tossed into the tunnel ahead once a rat falls.

The best tunnel rats have a stubborn will to survive. With a little luck and a lot of determination, these characters train themselves on the job. They learn to spot and disarm traps, for they believe that is a better course than simply stepping into them and setting them off. They learn to move with stealth and to keep hidden so that they may see enemies before they are seen. They learn to climb, to hunt, to fight, to find their way in the most confusing tunnels, for to do less is to fail at the task their chiefs have given them.

Of course, some decide that they do not like being unappreciated. These individuals leave their tribes in order to find fame and fortune. They sell their skills to those who need them, often joining adventuring parties about to embark on an underground quest.

Tunnel rats are extremely self-sufficient. They are almost supernaturally silent, appearing from the shadows without warning when the rest of their party least expects them. They are not easy to like, and they seldom make good friends, but they are invaluable when exploring the regions below the earth.

Weapon Proficiencies: Members of this kit must take the short sword proficiency. The other slot can be filled from the weapons usable by thieves.

Nonweapon Proficiencies:

- Bonus Proficiencies: Close-quarter fighting.
- Recommended, General: Alertness, danger sense, direction sense, hiding, navigation (underground), rope use, survival (underground).
- Recommended, Warrior: Endurance.
- Recommended, Priest: None.
- Recommended, Wizard: None.
- Recommended, Rogue: Jumping, tightrope walking.
- Forbidden: None.

Equipment: Tunnel rats can use and purchase any equipment and armor normally available to thieves. They should purchase basic survival equipment, including ropes, pitons, tools, food and water, etc.

Special Benefits: Tunnel rats receive a +5% bonus to their initial *find/remove traps, move silently,* and *climb walls* skills.

Special Hindrances: Tunnel rats have a –10% penalty to their *pick pocket* skill and a –5% penalty to their *read languages* skill.

Wealth Options: Each member of this kit begins play with 1d6 × 10 gp.

Shadow

Shadows are humanoid assassins. They have made their way in the world by killing others for profit. While many have private codes, others hire themselves out to the highest bidder. Shadows have a reputation for being competent, cold-blooded, and extremely efficient. Thus, when they no longer actively take commissions, they tend to drift into related activities: spying, bounty hunting, and the like.

Shadow player characters are extremely rare, but they might join adventuring parties with similar interests and goals. They are loners by nature, however, and seldom stay with a group for long.

Requirements: Shadows can be of the following races: bugbears, bullywugs, gnolls, flinds, goblins, hobgoblins, kobolds, lizard men, mongrelmen, ogre magi, orcs, or half-orcs. Either gender may become shadows. The

character must have minimum Strength and Dexterity scores of 12, and a minimum Intelligence of 11 to choose this kit. Shadows can be of any non-good alignment.

Role: Shadows are spies, assassins, and enforcers. Most leave their tribes to practice their profession in the outside world. Shadows earn their name from the way they live. Most are unseen until they strike, maintaining a low profile even when not on a job.

Most assassin guilds have at least one humanoid shadow on their rolls. They are saved for special assignments and for specific clients who favor their dark ways. Active shadows are proficient at stealth and killing, and spend much of their time honing their fighting skills to a fine edge in anticipation of the next assignment. Most are cool, calculating killing machines, and display a frightening lack of emotion when accomplishing their jobs.

Player character shadows are nearly always of neutral alignment and have often retired to general adventuring. Those still active as assassins often see themselves as agents of the forces of justice, the balance, tribal law, or some other principle. They consider the deaths they cause as justifiable evils, and only take commissions that fall into this category.

Weapon Proficiencies: Shadows may select any one-handed weapon, any weapon available to thieves, plus others appropriate to their profession (*e.g.:* blowgun, etc.).

Nonweapon Proficiencies:

• Bonus Proficiencies: Disguise.

• Recommended, General: Acting, alertness, begging, danger sense, hiding observation, voice mimicry.

• Recommended, Warrior: Hunting, intimidation, tracking.

• Recommended, Priest: Reading/writing.

• Recommended, Wizard: None.

• Recommended, Rogue: Blind-fighting, close-quarter fighting, information gathering, jumping, tumbling.

• Forbidden: None.

Equipment: Shadows can use all types of deadly equipment, but they are limited to the armor types available to other thieves, plus shields. Shadows do not make use of poison. They prefer to eliminate their targets with weapon and combat skills.

Special Benefits: When attacking with surprise, a shadow kills the victim if a hit is scored and the victim fails a saving throw vs. death; provided the victim has hit dice less than or equal to the shadow's. Otherwise, damage equal to a backstab is inflicted.

Special Hindrances: All thief abilities except *backstabbing* are rated two levels less than those of a thief of equal level. This means that all initial thief abilities except *hear noise* have an additional −10% penalty.

Wealth Options: Each shadow begins play with 2d6 × 10 gp. This sum represents all that remains of a shadow's last pay.

Humanoid Bard

Humanoid bards are basically humanoid versions of the human and half-elf bard. They follow all of the rules which apply to normal bards, though they have some special differences that separate them from the bards everyone knows. Unlike a true bard, who is a jack-of-all trades, humanoid bards (with some exceptions) normally focus on a particular brand of entertainment. Many sing, some dance, some act or tumble. A few even create and recite poetry. While most humanoid bards attempt to appeal to their particular audience, some (like mongrelmen bards) labor to create art that few other races can appreciate.

Requirements: Aarakocra, centaurs, flinds, mongrelmen, satyrs, voadkyn, and wemics can choose the bard kit. All must have a minimum Dexterity and Intelligence of 13. Most must have a minimum Charisma of 15. Mongrelman bards must have a minimum Charisma of 15 among their own kind. Humanoid bard alignment must be at least partially neutral.

Role: While all humanoid races have entertainers and storytellers, only a select few can produce characters which come close to the true bard class. These humanoid bards produce beautiful and inspiring ballads and songs (at least as far as other members of their race is concerned), and some even learn to grasp the intricate tastes of other cultures. In their own communities, humanoid bards are the keepers of tribal history, the chroniclers of important events, and the ambassadors to other tribes. In human society, they are more often entertainers, tugging a wide variety of emotions out of their audiences in exchange for profit, food, or shelter.

Even the best humanoid bards are often considered funny by humans and demihumans. Though this pains these artists, they accept their lot and try to make the best of it. Once in a rare while they are able to get across a message besides humor, but these flares of brilliance which cross over racial boundaries are fleeting indeed.

Humanoid bards make excellent adventuring companions, using their entertaining skills to brighten moods and inspire confidences. They have a variety of proficiencies to call upon, and while not as versatile as true bards, what skills and abilities they do have make them fairly formidable and extremely helpful.

Weapon Proficiencies: Humanoid bards are restricted as to weapons carried by thieves.

Nonweapon Proficiencies:
• Bonus Proficiencies: Local history.
• Required Proficiency: musical instrument and one of the following: chanting, dancing, juggling, poetry, singing.
• Recommended, General: Acting, artistic ability, chanting, craft instrument, crowd working, dancing, drinking, eating, etiquette, fortune telling, languages (modern), poetry, rope use, voice mimicry, whistling/humming.
• Recommended, Warrior: Any.
• Recommended, Priest: Any, except spellcraft.

• Recommended, Wizard: Any, except spellcraft.
• Recommended, Rogue: Any.
• Forbidden: Spellcraft. Humanoid bards never learn this proficiency.

Equipment: Humanoid bards may purchase any type of armor up to and including chain mail, and any equipment (except shields).

Special Benefits: Humanoid bards can influence the reactions of groups of NPCs like true bards. NPCs not of the bard's race receive a +3 bonus to their saving throw. NPCs of the bard's race have a –2 penalty to their saves.

Members of this kit can inspire and rally their companions with heroic songs and tales. This takes four rounds to complete, at the end of which time those who heard the inspiration (within a 10-foot radius of the humanoid bard) receive one of the following benefits (as decided by the bard): +1 to attack rolls; +1 to saving throws; +2 to morale. Members of the bard's race receive an additional +1 bonus. The chosen effect lasts one round per level of the bard. Companions who are actively engaged in battle cannot be inspired.

The humanoid bard can counter opposing sound-based attacks. This benefit can be used against songs, chants, wails, and magical commands or suggestions. This ability requires intense concentration, as per the bard rules in the *Player's Handbook*.

The humanoid bard has a 5% chance per level to identify the general purpose and function of any magical item.

Special Hindrances: Humanoid bards do have any spellcasting abilities. When attempting to entertain groups not of their own race, humanoid bards suffer a –3 penalty to all proficiency checks. Mongrelman bards can only affect such crowds negatively.

Wealth Options: Humanoid bards initially receive 3d6 × 5 gp to purchase equipment.

Humanoid characters have different proficiencies available to them than other character races because of the cultures and societies in which they live. In this chapter, all of the proficiencies available to starting humanoids have been gathered into one master table. This table includes all of the proficiencies listed in the *Player's Handbook,* as well as selected proficiencies from the other books in the *PHBR* series. Those listed in **boldface** type are new to this book and are explained in the text.

Italicized proficiencies require the player to record a specific topic or area covered by the proficiency. For example, if a goblin PC takes animal training, he must specify a type of animal, such as a worg. This would be recorded as Animal Training (Worg). Additional slots can be used to improve the specified proficiency or to gain a new area of expertise, like Animal Training (Hawk).

Those proficiencies marked with an asterisk (*) are from one of the other PHBR books, though they might fall under a different grouping than those listed here. They are explained briefly in this book for ease of reference. **Important Note:** The description given here for Alertness replaces the description in the *Complete Thief's Handbook.*

Proficiencies and Specialization

As explained in the *Player's Handbook,* a weapon proficiency measures a character's knowledge and training with a specific weapon. All of the weapons listed on Table 44 of the *Player's Handbook* are available to all humanoid races, unless otherwise stated in the initial racial weapon proficiencies detailed in Chapter Two. The new weapons described in Chapter Seven of this book are also open to many of the humanoid races. Single-class humanoid fighters can specialize according to the rules in the *Player's Handbook* for weapon specialization.

Table 4: Nonweapon Proficiency Groups

General

Proficiency	Slots Req'd.	Relevant Ability	Check Mod.
Acting*	1	Cha	−1
Agriculture	1	Int	0
Alertness*	1	Wis	+1
Animal Handling	1	Wis	−1
Animal Noise*	1	Wis	−1
Animal Training	1	Wis	0
Artistic Ability	1	Wis	0
Begging*	1	Cha	Special
Blacksmithing	1	Str	0
Brewing	1	Int	0
Carpentry	1	Str	0
Chanting*	1	Cha	+2
Cheesemaking	1	Int	0
Cobbling	1	Dex	0
Cooking	1	Int	0
Craft Instrument *	2	Dex	−2
Crowd Working*	1	Cha	+2
Dancing	1	Dex	0
Danger Sense	2	Wis	+1
Direction Sense	1	Wis	+1
Drinking	1	Con	0
Eating	1	Con	0
Etiquette	1	Cha	0
Fast-talking*	1	Cha	Special
Fire-building	1	Wis	−1
Fishing	1	Wis	−1
Fortune Telling*	2	Cha	+2
Heraldry	1	Int	0
Hiding	2	Int	−1
Languages, Modern	1	Int	0
Leatherworking	1	Int	0
Looting*	1	Dex	0
Mining	2	Wis	−3
Observation*	1	Int	0
Poetry*	1	Int	−2
Pottery	1	Dex	−2
Riding, Airborne	2	Wis	−2
Riding, Land-based	1	Wis	+3
Rope Use	1	Dex	0
Seamanship	1	Dex	+1

Seamstress/Tailor	1	Dex	−1
Singing	1	Cha	0
Stonemasonry	1	Str	−2
Swimming	1	Str	0
Voice Mimicry*	2	Cha	Special
Weather Sense	1	Wis	−1
Weaving	1	Int	−1
Whistling/ Humming*	1	Dex	+2
Winemaking	1	Int	0

Warrior

Proficiency	Slots Req'd.	Relevant Ability	Check Mod.
Animal Lore	1	Int	0
Armorer	2	Int	−2
Blind-fighting	2	NA	NA
Bowyer/Fletcher	1	Dex	−1
Charioteering	1	Dex	+2
Close-quarter Fighting	2	Dex	0
Endurance	2	Con	0
Gaming	1	Cha	0
Hunting	1	Wis	−1
Intimidation*	1	Str/Cha	0
Natural Fighting	2	Str	+1
Mountaineering	1	NA	NA
Navigation	1	Int	−2
Running	1	Con	−6
Set Snares	1	Dex	−1
Survival	2	Int	0
Tracking	2	Wis	0
Weaponsmithing	3	Int	−3
Wild Fighting	2	Con	0

Priest

Proficiency	Slots Req'd.	Relevant Ability	Check Mod.
Ancient History	1	Int	−1
Astrology	2	Int	0
Engineering	2	Int	−3
Healing	2	Wis	−2
Herbalism	2	Int	−2
Languages, Ancient	1	Int	0
Local History	1	Cha	0

Musical Instrument	1	Dex	−1
Navigation	1	Int	−2
Reading/Writing	1	Int	+1
Religion	1	Wis	0
Spellcraft	1	Int	−2

Rogue

Proficiency	Slots Req'd.	Relevant Ability	Check Mod.
Acting*	1	Cha	−1
Ancient History	1	Int	−1
Appraising	1	Int	0
Blind-fighting	2	NA	NA
Close-quarter Fighting	2	Dex	0
Disguise	1	Cha	−1
Forgery	1	Dex	−1
Gaming	1	Cha	0
Gem Cutting	2	Dex	−2
Information Gathering*		Int	Special
Juggling	1	Dex	−1
Jumping	1	Str	0
Local History	1	Cha	0
Musical Instrument	1	Dex	−1
Reading Lips	2	Int	−2
Set Snares	1	Dex	−1
Tightrope Walking	1	Dex	0
Tumbling	1	Dex	0
Ventriloquism	1	Int	−2

Wizard

Proficiency	Slots Req'd.	Relevant Ability	Check Mod.
Ancient History	1	Int	−1
Astrology	2	Int	0
Engineering	2	Int	−3
Gem Cutting	2	Dex	−2
Herbalism	2	Int	−2
Languages, Ancient	1	Int	0
Navigation	1	Int	−2
Reading/Writing	1	Int	+1
Religion	1	Wis	0
Spellcraft	1	Int	−2

Nonweapon Proficiencies

New proficiencies and existing proficiencies which do not appear in the *Player's Handbook* are described below. Those not described can be found in the *Player's Handbook*.

Acting

This proficiency allows a character to skillfully portray various roles, often as an entertainment. It can also be used to enhance a disguise. If a character has both acting and disguise proficiencies, the check for either is made with a +1 bonus.

Proficiency checks are required only if the actor must portray a particularly difficult role or is attempting to "ad lib" without rehearsal.

Alertness*

This proficiency allows a character to instinctively notice and recognize signs of a disturbance in the immediate vicinity. This ability reduces a character's chance of being surprised by 1 if he makes a successful proficiency check. (Note that this replaces the description of this proficiency in the *Complete Thief's Handbook.*)

Animal Noise

A character with this proficiency can imitate the noises made by various animals. A successful check means the character's noise cannot be distinguished from that of the actual animal, except by magical means.

A failed check produces a sound that varies from the animal's in some slight way. Those who are very familiar with the animal will recognize the intended mimicry at once. Other characters must make successful Wisdom checks to determine if they also realize the animal noise is an imitation.

Begging

Begging serves two functions. First, it allows characters to pose convincingly as beggars (and many humanoids in civilized areas spend some time begging for a living). Success in this function is automatic and no checks must be made. Second, it allows the character to earn a minimal daily income. To use this proficiency to earn money, it must be used in an area where people are present.

The following modifiers are suggested to the DM as guidelines. They do not take into account the wealth of a particular locale, just the population density. Impoverished regions might have greater negative modifiers, as might certain affluent areas with long traditions or great reputations for stinginess.

Begging Modifiers

Locale	Modifier
Uninhabited/Wilderness	Failure
Countryside	–7
Hamlet, Village	–5
Town	–2
City	0

A successful check enables a character to beg for enough money, goods or services to meet his basic needs (a little food and drink, a place to sleep). Begging cannot force PCs to give away money. Players are always free to decide how generous their characters are.

Blind-fighting*

See the *Player's Handbook* for full details on this proficiency. In general terms, this proficiency reduces the penalty for fighting while blinded from –4 to –2. It similarly reduces the penalty for fighting invisible opponents. Because many humanoids have infravision, this proficiency is not usually as useful for humanoids as it is for humans.

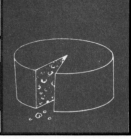

Chanting

Chanting is used to keep fellow workers or soldiers in pace. Proficiency checks are used to determine the effectiveness of a character's chanting.

Successful checks mean that those who can hear the chanting character become slightly hypnotized by the rhythmic sound, causing the time spent on arduous, repetitive tasks to pass quickly. The DM can, at his option, adjust results for forced marching, rowing, digging, and other similar tasks accordingly.

Cheesemaking

This proficiency allows the character who has it to expertly create cheese from the curds of soured milk. A proficiency check is required only when attempting to prepare a truly magnificent wheel of cheese as a special gift or for a special celebration.

Close-quarter Fighting

Humanoids with this proficiency have learned to fight in the cramped confines of dungeons and underground lairs. In such locations, or in other extremely close fighting conditions, characters armed with bludgeoning or piercing weapons (or their own natural weapons) receive a +2 bonus to attack rolls. Slashing weapons cannot be used in close-quarter fighting. This bonus is not cumulative with wild-fighting.

A successful proficiency check at the start of combat yields this bonus. Failure means the humanoid fights normally.

Craft Instrument

Characters with this proficiency must state which type of instrument they are skilled at crafting: wind, stringed, percussion, or keyboard. A slot must be used to gain each additional type of instrument the character wishes to be skilled at crafting. A total of four slots used in this proficiency grants a character the title of "master craftsman" who can craft instruments of all forms.

Characters must buy material equal to one quarter of the instrument's sale value. Wind and percussion instruments require 1d6 days of crafting, stringed instruments 2d8 days, and keyboard instruments 3d10 days. Each day of work requires 10 full hours spent crafting the instrument. If craftsman tools (cost 25 gp, weight 5 pounds) are not available, all times are doubled.

The crafted instrument's quality is determined by a final proficiency check. A failed check creates an instrument of poor quality, while a success indicates good quality. A natural 20 indicates that the instrument does not work, while a natural 1 produces a masterpiece worth twice its normal value.

Simple repairs to instruments take only 1d4 hours and require no checks unless the proper tools are not available. Repairing severe damage requires 1d8 hours, and a successful proficiency check is necessary to complete the repairs.

Crowd Working

Characters with this proficiency are familiar with how to handle crowds. They are skilled at observing crowds and adjusting their behavior accordingly. Humanoids who normally have this skill include all types of humanoid entertainers, from bards and fortune tellers, to acrobats and pit fighters.

This skill also can be used to adjust the encounter reaction of a crowd. A successful proficiency check will alter the crowd's reaction by two levels (or convinces them to donate twice as much money to the entertainers as they normally would).

Danger Sense

This proficiency provides a humanoid character with a sixth sense which warns of impending danger. On a successful check, the character avoids a trap at the last second or realizes that opponents wait to ambush him due to a sudden warning tingle that cannot be ignored. Characters who make successful checks spot traps before blundering into them and receive initiative against hidden opponents. This proficiency does not work against opponents who are out in the open and making no attempt to hide their actions. Failure indicates that the character senses nothing out of the ordinary and play continues normally.

Drinking

This proficiency, and its companion proficiency, Eating, is important to many humanoids, including centaurs, satyrs, and wemics. A successful check indicates that the humanoid can consume up to twice as much as normal at one sitting. This will allow the humanoid to go twice as long without drink before beginning to suffer adverse effects. If alcoholic beverages are involved, a successful check allows the humanoid to consume twice as much before adverse effects begin to bother him.

Eating

Much like the drinking proficiency, this proficiency allows the humanoid to store up food. A successful check indicates that the humanoid can consume up to twice as much as normal. This allows the humanoid to go twice as long without food without suffering any adverse effects from hunger.

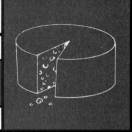

Fast-talking

Fast-talk is the art of distraction and conning NPCs. If a successful proficiency check is made, the fast-talker weaves a successful scam. Modifiers are based upon the Intelligence and Wisdom of the NPC target, as shown below. DMs may also introduce modifiers according to the difficulty or plausibility of what the character is attempting, as well as the racial preferences of the target character.

Fast-Talking Modifiers

Target's Intelligence	Mod.	Target's Wisdom	Mod.
3 or less	NA	3	-5
4-5	-3	4-5	-3
6-8	-1	6-8	-1
9-12	0	9-12	0
13-15	+1	13-15	+1
16-17	+2	16-17	+3
18	+3	18	+5
19	+5	19+	NA
20+	NA		

Modifiers are cumulative. Targets of Intelligence 3 or less are so dim that attempts to fast-talk them fail automatically because they cannot follow what is being said. Targets with Intelligence of 20 or more or Wisdom of 19 or more are impervious to fast-talking.

Fortune Telling

Many humans and demihumans believe humanoids have mysterious powers and abilities. While many do have abilities which are strange and different, telling the future is not among them (except for the rare shaman or witch doctor). However, few members of other races know this, and that's where the fortune telling proficiency comes in.

With this proficiency, characters know a variety of methods for divining the future — and they are all fake. Humanoids with this skill employ odd-looking devices, sonorous oratory, or other methods to convince others that they are authentic soothsayers. Common methods include cards, palm reading, counting bumps, casting runes, examining animal entrails, and more. Humanoid fortune tellers put on a good show, then proclaim whatever prediction they want. This is done to gain money from the gullible, to impress other humanoids, or even to substitute for a true diviner when none are available. Humanoids are extremely superstitious, after all, and many tribes are happy to have the services of a fake when no true shaman is available. Without the fortune teller, many tribes might be paralyzed by their fear of the unknown.

A successful proficiency check indicates that the target believes the fortune. If it fails, the sham is discovered or the fortune is simply not believed. Failure for a character trying to convince his tribe of his powers could prove deadly — for the fake! The fast-talking modifiers can be used if the DM desires. Note that PCs are never forced to believe a prediction regardless of the roll.

> **Optional Rule:** As an optional rule, the prediction made by the fortune teller actually comes true on a roll of a natural 1 (or some other number chosen secretly by the DM before the check is made).

Hiding

Hiding is the ability to instinctively select the best hiding place under nearly any condition. Humanoids who make successful checks can virtually disappear from view. Success is determined by modifiers based upon the Intelligence of the character being hidden from. This proficiency operates independently of any natural camouflage or hiding ability the humanoid might already have.

Hiding Modifiers

Opponent's Intelligence	Modifier
3 or less	-5
4-5	-3
6-8	-1
9-12	0
13-15	+1
16-17	+2
18	+3
19	+5
20+	+7

Information Gathering

Through the use of this proficiency, a humanoid character can gain information about a specific person, place or thing. In appropriate circumstances, a character will be aware of major rumors circulating around a roguish or humanoid area. With a successful check, specific information can be gleaned.

The following modifiers adjust the check:

Characters' reaction adjustments (based on Charisma) will benefit or penalize the roll, assuming contact with intelligent beings is involved in the search.

Thieves' guild members receive a +2 bonus as they have the resources of the entire guild at their disposal. Similarly, outside of towns and cities, certain humanoid characters may receive the same bonus if they have similar contacts (satyrs and swanmays have woodland creatures, a goblin may be able to get information from a goblin tribe, etc.).

When outside friendly territory, specific information suffers at least a –3 penalty.

Money or treasure is required. Any time a proficiency check is required to gather information, the character must make a small investment of money or treasure or suffer an additional penalty of –3. Humans prefer money, and a total of 1d10 gp is typical. Other races may want some other type of treasure (food, magical item, shiny trinket, etc.). The investment is lost whether or not the desired information is found.

Intimidation

This proficiency allows characters to bend others to their will through fear tactics. NPCs who are intimidated are quite likely to do as they are told. They are also very likely to harbor much resentment against the character that intimidates them. NPCs will keep their resentment hidden until the first opportunity to avenge their pride arises.

Intimidation can be attempted with either Strength or Charisma. Strength indicates a threat of immediate bodily injury. Charisma uses more subtle threats which need not be physical in nature.

Player characters are never required to submit to intimidation.

Looting

This proficiency represents a knack for grabbing the best loot in the shortest amount of time. A successful proficiency check allows a character to recognize and grab the most valuable combination of items that is feasible, given the situational limits of time and space.

Natural Fighting

This proficiency allows humanoids with natural weaponry (claws, fangs, tails, etc.) a +1 damage bonus on all natural weapon attacks. In addition, they receive a free natural attack beyond normal attacks they are allowed. A successful proficiency check must be made at the beginning of combat to gain the benefits of this skill. Failure indicates that the benefits cannot be used for the duration of the battle.

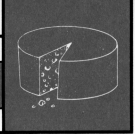

Observation

This proficiency represents a character's exceptionally acute powers of observation. DMs may ask for checks (or roll them secretly) whenever there is something slightly out of the ordinary. Characters with this proficiency have their chances of finding secret doors increased to 2 in 6, and concealed doors to 3 in 6. This proficiency covers all the senses.

Poetry

This proficiency includes the skills necessary to recite poetry and judge its quality. It also indicates that a character has a repertoire of poems memorized for recital at any time. No check is required for a normal recital.

If the character can read and write, original poems can be written. A successful check indicates that the poem is of above average quality.

Voice Mimicry

Voice mimicry is the art of convincingly imitating the voices of other people. It is a very demanding skill, requiring intense training and practice.

A character with voice mimicry can imitate any accent he has heard. Success is automatic unless confronted by those who speak the mimicked accent (which then requires a check with a +2 modifier).

It is more difficult to imitate a specific person's voice. Characters can only attempt to imitate voices they have heard. A proficiency check must be made to determine if the imitation is detected. Success is certain if the listener is a stranger to the mimicked character. There is no modifier if trying to fool an acquaintance, –2 to fool a friend, –5 a close friend, and –7 for extremely close friends and relatives.

Whistling/Humming

Characters with this proficiency are exceptional whistlers and hummers. They can produce tunes as captivating as most songs. If a successful check is made, the character knows any particular tune in question. If he also has the animal lore proficiency, he can mimic any bird call he has ever heard.

Adventurers also use this proficiency to communicate with each other. This type of communication is only possible among the characters who have this proficiency. If two or more characters with this proficiency make successful checks, a single concept can be communicated between them.

Wild Fighting

Characters with this proficiency employ an extremely unorthodox and unpredictable fighting style. Wild fighting is ferocious and deadly, without any grace or discipline. It is also extremely tiring, as part of its nature is that it focuses every bit of energy a character has into the attack.

The benefits are in the number of attacks the character gets and in the amount of damage attacks inflict. A wild-fighting character gets one more attack per round than normally entitled to. All damage rolls for attacks that hit receive a +3 bonus.

However, when wild fighting, a character's attack rolls also are reduced by 3. Also the attacker's armor class is penalized by 3, making it easier to hit him.

To use wild fighting, a character must make a successful proficiency check at the start of combat. A failure means that the character receives only the penalties of the proficiency and none of the benefits.

Wild fighting can only be used twice per day, as it is extremely tiring. After a battle ends, the

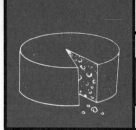

wild fighter must rest for one hour before he can again call on the proficiency. Resting means doing nothing but resting or engaging in light travel (riding a slow-moving horse, etc.). If the character must walk, he cannot use the proficiency until four hours have passed. Without this rest, a tired character suffers a –3 penalty to all proficiency checks, a –5 to armor class, a –5 to THAC0, and a –3 from damage rolls. These penalties are in effect until the full resting period has elapsed.

Winemaking

This proficiency allows characters to create wine from the fermented juice of grapes or other plants and fruits well enough to make a living at it. The character will always succeed to some extent; proficiency checks are only required when attempting to prepare a truly magnificent wine as a special gift or for a special celebration.

Players who decide to create humanoid characters should have good role-playing as their ultimate goal. Avoid choosing a humanoid character type by its benefits, hindrances, or how powerful it can become. Strange humanoid beliefs, uncivilized habits, the reactions of others, and the clash of human and humanoid cultures are a few of the many hooks upon which a humanoid personality can be hung. Humanoids are best viewed as unusual personas through which character and story development can take place.

This chapter gives suggestions to help players create humanoid characters that are well-rounded and fun to play, with an eye toward keeping any "unfair" advantages in check. Further, some of these suggestions can be used by the Dungeon Master to restore campaign balance if a character gets off track.

The number of humanoid races given in this book require that suggestions be of a general nature. It is up to the players and the DM to make them work in the context of a particular race of humanoids in a particular campaign setting. Examples are provided, but space limitations make covering every possible combination impossible.

Life as a Humanoid

For the majority of humanoids, life is lived in a clan or tribe. These tribes are made up of loosely-related families which are led by chiefs. The chiefs are normally the strongest and most able fighters of the group, though some tribes turn to elders and thinkers for leadership. Life in the tribes is hard. The wilderness does not give up sustenance easily, and tribesmen must constantly work to survive. This work could be hunting, gathering, fishing, craftworking, scavenging, mining, farming, raiding, plundering, or some combination of these, depending on the tribal race, alignment, and nature.

In most cases, a humanoid tribe will be less civilized, less advanced, and less established than its human or demihuman counterpart.

Lawful tribes prefer stability and order. They organize themselves in all endeavors, setting up rules to cover all aspects of life and society. For these tribes to function, there must be an obvious and unchanging chain of leader-ship. In lawful evil tribes, there are severe laws and harsh punishments. These are not established to provide justice, but to preserve the stability of the tribe.

Good tribes cherish life. They are more concerned with finding ways to make their tribes prosper than in competing for social positions (at least in openly hostile ways). Life is more positive among these tribes, though not necessarily easier.

On the evil side, might makes right and fear keeps the masses in line. Change is still sudden and frequent, but it tends to be violent and deadly in nature. Many evil humanoids are nomads, though some do set up semi-permanent settlements when they find a location that fills their survival needs and greedy habits. Once settled, they quickly deplete the location of the resources that attracted them. They treat the land and its bounties as they treat each other — with little respect and as something to be exploited. When a region no longer suits their needs (due to their own overindulgences and uncaring practices), these humanoids move on in search of new spoils and plunder.

Chaotics share a frivolous or capricious nature. Change is often welcome, or and even sought out on a daily basis. Few activities are organized beyond the minimum level necessary to accomplish a given task. Some chaotic cultures seem to find even this level of organization difficult; disagreements and in-fighting often result.

On the good side, chaotics like to manage their own affairs. They may bow to a single leader, but prefer to do as they please so long as they stay within broad behavioral guidelines. Even though they love independence and despise rules, many chaotic and good humanoids come to love nature and respect its

bounties. Many form such close ties with their environments as to become caretakers of a sort. Nature may be used, but never abused.

In a chaotic evil tribe, life is even more of a struggle. Not only must tribe members battle the elements, nature and other tribes, they often fight among themselves for positions of leadership and the pick of loot. Life is cheap among them, for killing is usually the easiest method of advancement up a tribe's social and political ladder. This may also be true in other evil and neutral communities, but such violence is usually less random.

Tribal Life

All humanoid tribes share a fear of the supernatural, and anything they do not understand falls into this category. This results in superstitions which fill their days and nights, and dictate the way in which they conduct their lives. Superstitions serve to reinforce the opinion that humanoids are primitive savages, though few humans get to know them well enough to see their beliefs in practice.

Tribal life starts in ernest when humanoid children are old enough to understand and participate in the world around them. Most humanoids relegate different roles and tasks to males and females, and children are immediately immersed in the social order so that they grow to know and embrace it. They receive instruction, usually in informal settings, learning what they need to survive and prosper by observing, participating, and some training. The level of training depends on the nature, disposition and societal level of the race in question. During their early years, children spend most of their time with females and shamans. Here they learn the legends and beliefs of their tribe, as well as many of the social rules they will need in tribal life. Children begin to work as soon as they are able, at first helping with whatever domestic activities the tribe engages in and eventually moving on

to their life's work.

When they near maturity, humanoids apprentice themselves to adults in order to learn the trades of the tribe. This apprenticeship can be formal, as in the case of orcs, or extremely informal where younger tribe members learn through observation and proximity as opposed to specific instruction. In cases where there is even a hint of formality, tribal shamans, witch doctors, and chiefs assign children to specific trades (hunting, raiding, mining, fighting, etc.). They make their decisions based upon their observations of the children, the needs of the tribe, the social rank of a child's parents, and by reading the signs and omens associated with a particular child.

From an early age, a humanoid's role in the tribe is set. Most prefer this arrangement, for it gives them a function and purpose. A select few desire to find their own path, and these inevitably are weeded out through violence, cast out by decree, or leave of their own accord to make their own lives. These are the outcasts, the hermits, and the adventurers. The few that find their way into human society are the ones we are most concerned with.

Social and Racial Disadvantages

Humanoids start out with disadvantages in non-humanoid societies. All but the most enlightened civilizations consider humanoids to be monsters. Centuries of competition, violence and warfare has made humans and humanoids natural enemies, striving for the same resources. Truth became legends, and legends bred fears that haunt both sides, filling their heads with truths, half-truths, and lies. But humans are more numerous, more advanced, more established. They are winning the battle of dominion over the world. For better or for worse, though there are still vast stretches of untamed wilderness, it has become a human world.

For this reason, humanoids find themselves at a disadvantage. When they leave their tribes

to find their own path in the world, it inevitably crosses into human civilization. Humanoids are strangers to human civilization (or even demihuman, for that matter). They know it only as something out of tribal legends, or from the scary stories told around the evening fire, or from the skirmishes their tribe may have had with a town or village in the past. They do not know the customs. They do not know the social etiquette. They probably do not understand many of the "advanced" conveniences that dominate civilized life.

It is up to players and DMs to work together to stress a humanoid's unfamiliarity with civilization. In the same way as a DM describes newly-discovered magical items by their appearance without giving away any details, so too must a DM describe the items and practices of civilization. From a humanoid's point of view — clothing, armor, weapons, tools, utensils — everything is strange, wondrous, frightening, and unknown. The trappings which players normally take for granted should become new and

mysterious to humanoid characters.

For example, Breeka the aarakocra enters a human town for the first time. What are the strange wooden caves that humans go in and out of? Why do those humans shake hands? Or press their lips together? Or give shiny objects to one another? And why is that human yelling because Breeka ate the pig in front of his wooden cave? Breeka, who has never before encountered a human town, finds herself surrounded by unusual trappings and strange practices which she will have to spend time getting to understand. While players can roleplay a lack of understanding concerning human social customs, it is up to the DM to keep in mind that the most obvious thing to a human or demihuman is probably a mystery to the humanoid, and to describe encounter scenes accordingly.

Beyond the social disadvantages which humanoids face when dealing with communities beyond their own, there are also racial discriminations to deal with. Because most

humans and demihumans see humanoids as little more than monsters, there will be extreme prejudices directed at them. Humanoids will be watched almost constantly when they enter a human community — if they are allowed to enter at all. Many towns and cities will have laws forbidding the entry of humanoids. They will be stopped at the gates, turned away, or even attacked. Humans fear that a humanoid has come to scout out the community for attack, or seeks to cause some other type of trouble. They believe that humanoids eat humans (and some do), and who wants a monster walking on the streets of town?

Many inns have rules against serving humanoids. Shops refuse to deal with them. Local authorities stay close, watching for the least sign of trouble. They have no qualms about arresting and locking up humanoids that so much as look at a human the wrong way — and banishment or confinement are the nicest things they might do to them. Mobs form quickly in the presence of humanoids, ready to take torch and pitchfork to a monster in order to protect their loved ones. Again, it is up to the DM to enforce this disadvantage. Even the most powerful humanoid PC will be hard-pressed to find a place to rest or buy supplies in a hate-filled, fearful town. If a humanoid is allowed to operate as any normal PC as far as NPCs are concerned, then a great role-playing challenge is lost.

Another problem facing humanoids in human communities deals with the fact that things are built in human dimensions. Doors and rooms are made to accommodate human heights and widths. Chairs and beds are made to hold human weights. Even most transportation modes, such as horses and wagons, cannot sustain large-sized humanoids. This is not a problem for the man-sized humanoids, but tiny-, small-, and large-sized humanoids must learn to live in a human-sized world.

Humanoid Traits

Humanoids have a number of monstrous traits. These may be perfectly normal and acceptable in their own society, but in human society they are gross and frightening. These traits provide bonuses or penalties to PC actions. Every humanoid has at least one trait that is shared by every member of its race (this are given in the humanoid's entry in Chapter Two). The DM may also require humanoid PCs to roll for 1-2 additional monstrous traits, if desired.

Bestial Appetite 1: Humanoid has the appetite of a large beast; must consume twice as much food as a normal human at every meal or suffer a –1 penalty to Strength and Constitution scores.

Bestial Appetite 2: Humanoid has the appetite of a huge beast; must consume three times as much food as a normal human at every meal or suffer a –2 penalty to Strength and Constitution scores.

Bestial Appetite 3: Humanoid has the appetite of a gargantuan beast; must consume four times as much food as a normal human at every meal or suffer a –3 penalty to Strength and Constitution scores.

Bestial Fear: Humanoid has a beast's natural fear of a given thing (PC or DM's choice). In presence of this thing, the humanoid must make a save vs. spell or suffer effects as per a wizard's *fear* spell.

Bestial Habits: Humanoid has a habit that resembles the behavior of a beast as opposed to the behavior of a civilized person. These cause a –2 penalty to reaction rolls.

Bestial Intelligence 1: Humanoid has a reduced Intelligence score of –1; maximum 14, minimum 3.

Bestial Intelligence 2: Humanoid has a reduced Intelligence score of –3; maximum 12, minimum 3.

Bestial Intelligence 3: Humanoid has a reduced Intelligence score of –5, maximum 9, minimum 2.

Bestial Odor: A bad smell; -2 penalty to reaction checks.

Bestial Rage: A monstrous temper; madly attacks nearest character for 1d4 rounds if it fails a Wisdom check. The rage should have a specific trigger.

Bestial Speech: Humanoid has a speech pattern that includes bestial sounds; –2 penalty to reaction checks.

Bestial Thirst 1: Humanoid has the thirst of a large beast; must consume twice as much liquid in a day or suffer a –1 penalty to Strength and Constitution scores.

Bestial Thirst 2: Humanoid has the thirst of a huge beast; must consume three times as much liquid in a day or suffer a –3 penalty to Strength and Constitution scores.

Bestial Thirst 3: Humanoid has the thirst of a gargantuan beast; must consume four times as much liquid in a day or suffer a –5 penalty to Strength and Constitution scores.

Light Sensitivity: Humanoid is sensitive to bright light; receives a –1 penalty to all attack rolls made in daylight or other bright light conditions.

Monstrous Appearance 1: Humanoid appears strange and frightening; –2 penalty to reaction checks.

Monstrous Appearance 2: Humanoid appears strange and frightening; –4 penalty to reaction checks.

Monstrous Appearance 3: Humanoid appears strange and frightening; –6 penalty to reaction checks.

Monstrous Craving: Humanoid sometimes craves a particular item (food, drink, or other), chosen jointly by the player and DM. When a monstrous craving occurs (not more than once a week), the humanoid has a –1 penalty to all ability and proficiency checks (cumulative per hour) until the craving is satisfied.

Monstrous Dexterity 1: Humanoid has enhanced Dexterity; +1 bonus to Dexterity score (minimum 6), –1 penalty to reaction checks.

Monstrous Dexterity 2: Humanoid has enhanced Dexterity; +2 bonus to Dexterity score (minimum 8), –1 penalty to reaction checks.

Monstrous Dexterity 3: Humanoid has enhanced Dexterity; +3 bonus to Dexterity score (minimum 10), –1 penalty to reaction checks.

Monstrous Hearing: Humanoid has keen hearing; can *hear noise* as a thief. Base score 25%; +25% at ages below middle age, +15% at middle age, +0% at old age, –15% at venerable age.

Monstrous Sight: Humanoid has keen vision; can see to a visibility range 50% greater than a normal human.

Monstrous Size: Humanoid is larger than others of his kind (either taller or wider); +1 bonus to Strength score, –3 penalty to reaction checks.

Monstrous Smell: Humanoid has sensitive sense of smell; +1 on surprise checks, –2 to saving throws against foul odors.

Monstrous Strength 1: Humanoid has great Strength; +1 bonus to Strength score (minimum 6), –1 penalty to reaction checks.

Monstrous Strength 2: Humanoid has great Strength; +3 bonus to Strength score (minimum 10), –2 penalty to reaction checks.

Monstrous Strength 3: Humanoid has great Strength; +5 bonus to Strength score (minimum 12), –3 penalty to reaction checks.

Monstrous Taste: Humanoid has a very sensitive sense of taste; +2 save vs. imbibed poisons.

Monstrous Touch: Humanoid has a very sensitive sense of touch; +5% success chance for delicate manipulations, –2 saving throw against physical pain or irritation.

Optional Rule: For every special advantage a humanoid has due to its racial type, it rolls for an extra monstrous trait. Additional traits may result in cumulative penalties. Thus, an aarakocra PC starts with bestial speech, then rolls for two more traits.

Campaign Complications

Table 19: Campaign Complications in the table section lists some of the more common problems which humanoid PCs face on a daily basis. These are presented as suggestions for Dungeon Masters to draw from when setting up campaigns containing humanoid PCs. All Dungeon Masters are urged to expand and customize these tables for their own campaigns. The more powerful a humanoid PC is, the more often a complication should arise. Experienced DMs need not use the tables directly, but can use them as reminders of the types of problems humanoids face in human civilizations.

The campaign complications are divided into two groups: wilderness and civilization. When humanoid player characters are outside of settlements, they will face the types of complications listed on the Wilderness table. In human or demihuman villages, towns, and cities, the complications they must deal with are those of civilization. A brief description of these complications follows.

Adventurers: The humanoid character has become the target of an adventuring party, and must somehow find a way to throw them off its trail. The reason for the adventurers' interest should be worked into the campaign plot.

Arrested: The humanoid is arrested for committing a crime, for suspicion of a crime, or just because the local authorities don't like its presence. Often, when a humanoid commits a crime, it does not know or understand the local laws and customs, or it has fallen prey to unscrupulous exploitation.

Banished: For inadvertently committing a crime or social blunder in human civilization, the humanoid is banished from the settlement by a local mob, militia, or adventuring party.

Captured: The humanoid is captured by those hostile to it and must escape or be rescued. This complication is often used in conjunction with another, such as Banished, Arrested, Slavers, etc.

Challenged: A human or demihuman NPC decides to impress his or her peers by challenging a humanoid PC to a duel or contest.

Cleric: A cleric takes an interest in the humanoid. This interest can be with an eye to befriend or convert the humanoid, or it can be of a negative nature — an evil cleric needs the humanoid for some foul purpose, or a good cleric decides to eradicate the monster.

Educational Limitation: The humanoid runs into a problem due to a lack of knowledge concerning the settlement currently being visited. This could do with reading or language, with a knowledge of laws or customs, or even with understanding the local currency.

Exploitation: An unscrupulous human (or demihuman) takes advantage of the humanoid while pretending to befriend him. Exploitation can be overt: slavery, selling a humanoid to the battle pits, turning a humanoid into a carnival sideshow exhibit; or it can be subtle: a swindler's con job, a human tricking the humanoid into fighting his enemies, etc.

Fear: Many humans and demihumans fear humanoids. To them, humanoids are nothing but foul monsters. In this type of complication, humanoids must deal with people who are deathly afraid of them.

Humanoids: Other humanoids appear to hinder the humanoid character. These can be members of the original tribe, others of the same race, or humanoids from a different race. If they are from a different race, they could be hostile to the character's racial type.

Hunters: Hunters cross the humanoid's path. They can be searching for that humanoid or for one of like race (to sell to a battle pit or wizard, for example) or they could be after other game entirely and then decide to focus on the humanoid. Hunters might be of any race.

Local Authorities: The local authorities (militia, town leaders) take an interest in the humanoid. They may want to keep an eye on the stranger, hire the humanoid to do a specific task, or they harass the humanoid to drive it away.

Mob: An angry mob gathers and comes after the humanoid. They could be motivated by something the humanoid did (or is believed to have done), or they could simply band together out of fear or hatred.

Monster: The humanoid wanders near a monster's lair, and the monster decides it wants the humanoid for some reason (food, slave, etc.).

Physical Limitation: The humanoid runs into something in human society which is a hinderance based on its size or body type (steep stairs, door or furniture too large or small, etc.)

Prejudice: The humanoid encounters severe prejudice or outright hatred. There may not be specific restrictions or laws, but humans can hinder and abuse humanoids by refusing to serve them, throwing garbage at them, calling them names, cursing them, or simply going out of their way to avoid them.

Restrictions: A restriction or law hinders the humanoid. Samples: no humanoid can be served at a particular shop or establishment; no humanoid can enter a particular part of the city; no humanoid can enter the city itself; no humanoid can talk to citizens, etc.

Rogue: A rogue exploits the humanoid (see Exploitation).

Sentenced to Death: A death sentence is a hard thing to live with, and humanoids often blunder into them. These should be used only rarely, and they will often become the focus of a particular adventure.

Slavers: Slavers, either humanoid or human, hunt the humanoid character. If captured, the character might be sold or taken back to the slavers' community and put to work.

Social Blunder: Due to a lack of understanding or knowledge concerning social customs, the humanoid makes a blunder. This can be mild and amusing, or major and unforgiven. Any action can become a social blunder, from a humanoid not knowing the proper way to respond to a greeting, to the humanoid using a tribal greeting (which may frighten, anger, or amuse the humans at whom it is directed).

Superstition: One of the humanoid's superstitions (see Chapter Six) comes into play at an inopportune moment.

Trait: A situation develops wherein one of the humanoid's monstrous traits causes a problem.

Travelers: Traveling humans or demihumans encounter the humanoid and react in one of several ways: hostile, friendly, suspicious, curious, fearful, etc. This is one way to bring the problems of cultural interaction to a humanoid character in the wilderness.

Warrior: A fighter type encounters the humanoid and decides to test his strength against it, banish it, drive it away, or take other "heroic" action — usually to the humanoid's dismay.

Wizard: A mage desires the humanoid. Usually, wizards need humanoids to get special spell components (which may come from the humanoid's dead body!), to help with a magical ceremony, or to undertake a quest for which they have unique talents.

A Mysterious World

Like the primitive ancestors of humans and demihumans, most humanoids still embrace the fears and wonders of the primordial world, a world that still exists in its simplest, most frightening form. To the humanoid, the world beyond his fire is unknown. All manner of creatures and supernatural beings roam these unknown regions, waiting to harm the humanoid who wanders too far from the fire's protective glow.

Even the most civilized humanoid will often use an elaborate system of safeguards that appear irrational to non-humanoids. For example, a forest kobold of Amn waking on his left side must immediately spit three times or suffer an unlucky day.

Many humanoid superstitions are outward manifestations of racial or cultural anxieties, but others have to do with the external powers of the world — the gods, spirits, and other supernatural beings that populate the campaign world. These powers must be bribed or charmed into leaving the humanoid alone, lest all manner of bad luck and suffering result.

Humans and demihumans might consider these practices to be outmoded, primitive, or even absurd, but most humanoids consider every such ritual to be of life-and-death importance. This belief stays with a humanoid character his whole life, no matter how many years he stays away from his tribe. Every superstition has a legend behind it and comes with a ready-made ritual for attracting beneficial influences and warding off malevolent ones. Thus, many humanoid characters remain perfectly at home in their beliefs, always on the lookout for signs and omens, ever ready with an oft-practiced ward.

Humans may well be uncomfortable around humanoids for any number of reasons, and many commoner folk definitely find the latter's constant reference to unseen forces unnerving. To the humanoid, however, it is just a way of life.

In a world that is often hostile, dangerous and extremely unpredictable, such humanoid superstitions offer some measure of comfort and control. Naming a fear goes far toward conquering it, or at least reducing it to a concrete thing that may be fought. When fear sweeps over humanoids, their superstitions provide assurance that they can influence their fate with simple, time-honored rituals.

Some rituals require simple actions such as gestures. Others need the additional power of a physical charm, such as a rabbit's foot or griffon's quill. Each charm has its own function; a humanoid may carry several different types of charms to ward off fear or bad luck. These charms may be worn openly or kept hidden until needed.

To humanoids, who often feel powerless in the face of nature, other races, and even their own kind, superstitions are almost a form of personal magic. This magic does not produce impressive displays of light and sound, nor does it strike opponents with deadly force. Instead, it helps a humanoid come to terms with the unknown. Each small ritual, either positive or negative in nature, is repeated over and over as a form of cause and effect. If kissing her sword once helped a female hobgoblin defeat an opponent, then she might have permanently adopted the kissing ritual in order to continue her good luck.

Superstitions in Game Terms

All humanoid player characters should have two or more superstitions that can affect play during the course of their adventures and campaigns. The first superstition is racial or tribal, common to all members of a particular humanoid race or tribe. (Suitable superstitions are listed in the humanoid racial entries in Chapter Two.) The second type of superstition is personal. A personal superstition can be selected by the player or rolled randomly on Table 18: General

Superstitions, located in the table section.

To determine how many personal superstitions a humanoid PC has, first find that character's prime requisite on the table below. Select or roll that many more superstitions from the General Superstitions table (as approved by the DM). Of all the PC's superstitions, one may be positive; the rest must be negative.

Table 5: Personal Superstitions

Prime Requisite Score	Number of Additional Superstitions
9-11	1
12-15	2
16+	3

Superstitions have two functions. First, they provide more hooks for building a humanoid PC's personality, thus providing more fuel for good role-playing. Second, they help or hinder a character in play, giving bonuses or penalties to dice rolls in encounters in which the superstition has manifested itself.

Using Superstitions in Play

A humanoid PC who encounters a manifestation of a superstition must make a Wisdom check at a –2 penalty. (The DM may increase the penalty depending on the nature of the manifestation. A particularly frightening superstition combined with a particularly powerful manifestation might have a penalty as high as –6.) Success or failure of the Wisdom check determines the effects on the PC, depending on whether the superstition is positive or negative.

Positive superstitions are manifestations of good luck. Using charms or gestures, the humanoid receives the benefits of benevolent forces. *Negative superstitions*, on the other hand, are manifestations of bad luck, ill will, and outright malevolence. Charms and gestures allow the humanoid to ward off these forces. Even if the charm or ges-

ture works, however, the fear generated by a close call with harmful forces may cause the humanoid to suffer some lesser penalties.

Positive superstition checks are made when the PC chooses when to call upon the power of his charm or gesture ritual.

Negative superstition checks must be made every time the superstition manifests itself.

Penalties and bonuses for superstitions are not cumulative. Only one type of penalty or bonus can be in effect in any given hour.

Success, Positive Superstition: A humanoid PC succeeding at a Wisdom check when a positive superstition manifests will receive a +2 bonus to all proficiency and ability checks, and a +1 bonus to all attack rolls. These benefits last for one hour and can only be gained once per day, no matter how often the superstition manifests itself.

Failure, Positive Superstition: A humanoid PC failing a Wisdom check receives no bonus or penalty. After one hour has passed, if the superstition manifests itself, the PC can make a Wisdom check, at a –4 penalty. If the check fails a second time, the PC can make one final attempt an hour later, at a –6 penalty. If this check also fails, the PC cannot try to gain the benefits of his positive superstition until 24 hours have passed — no matter how often the superstition manifests in his presence.

Success, Negative Superstition: A humanoid PC making a successful Wisdom check when a negative superstition manifests receives a –2 penalty to all proficiency and ability checks, and a –1 penalty to all attack rolls, due to the fear a negative superstition generates (failure is much more debilitating). These penalties last for one hour.

Failure, Negative Superstition: A humanoid PC failing a Wisdom check receives a –4 penalty to all proficiency and ability checks, and a –2 penalty to all attack rolls. These penalties are in effect for one hour.

Important Note: The superstitions suggested on Table 18: General Superstitions are presented in broad categories. They should be refined to a specific type of manifestation, a specific ritual for calling upon or warding off its effects, and an accompanying legend to make the superstition make sense.

For example, Hegral the female bugbear rolls a superstition dealing with noise. Her player decides that the superstition will be negative. It manifests itself as thunder. Whenever Hegral hears thunder, she must blink three times and spin once counterclockwise to ward off its evil effects. This superstition of thunder relates to the sound the bugbear God of Fear makes when passing from the Abyss to the Prime Material plane in search of a bugbear to carry off.

The Superstitions

The following suggested superstitions can be used to develop the categories provided on the General Superstitions table. Dungeon Masters and players can expand this list and create their own superstitions, using these as guidelines and springboards for other ideas.

Animal/Insect: A specific kind of animal or insect causes this superstition to manifest.

Armor: A specific type of armor, worn by an opponent, frightens or inspires the humanoid.

Cold: Sudden chills, fear of ice or snow, fear or positive belief in icy winds.

Color: Fear of a particular color, manifested in nature, on clothes, or in some other way.

Demihumans: The humanoid fears a specific demihuman race. The race is usually determined by the humanoid's racial preferences and hatreds.

Destiny: The humanoid has learned of his particular destiny from an oracle or fortune teller. Whenever this destiny seems to be

occurring, the humanoid receives either a negative or positive superstition. For example, a humanoid who was told she would die by a human's arrow will be fearful in the presence of human archers.

Dreams: A specific, recurring dream haunts or inspires a humanoid.

Elements: Air, earth, fire or water causes either fear or hope in a superstitious humanoid. In all cases, the humanoid should pick a specific manifestation of the element in question (swirling air, cracked earth, uncontrolled fire, foul water, etc.).

Gods: Humanoid suffers from a fear of a particular god, or looks for signs from a particular god as a manifestation of good luck.

Heat: Fear of hot flashes, of hot weather, of temperatures above a certain level.

Humanoids: A specific race of humanoids causes this superstition to manifest. Some humanoids are even afraid of others of their own kind due to the reasons why they left to become adventurers.

Magical Items: The humanoid fears a particular type of magical item. This can be general, for example a magical wand, or specific, as in a magical wand that casts *fireballs.*

Monsters: The humanoid fears a particular type of monster. This superstition can manifest either when the monster is present or when the humanoid sees signs of its passage. As a positive superstition, the monster in question can be the humanoid's patron creature.

Moon: Fear or positive belief in one of the stages of the moon (full, half, quarter, new).

Noise: A noise (which must be specifically identified) giving either a positive or negative manifestation.

Plants: A specific type of plant causes the humanoid's superstition to take effect. A humanoid could be afraid of red roses, but inspired by blooming lilies, for example.

Priests: Priests of a specific alignment or religion frighten or inspire the humanoid.

Reptiles: A specific type of reptile causes a humanoid's superstition to take effect. Reptiles include crocodiles, lizards, and snakes.

Sickness: The sight of a person or animal with a specific type of illness causes the humanoid to suffer a negative superstition. If the humanoid himself gets the illness, the effects of the negative superstition last until the illness is cured.

Specific Location: A specific location or location type (dark caves, twisted forests, babbling brooks, human villages, etc.) elicits fear in the humanoid.

Stars: Fear or positive belief in a particular star or constellation.

Storms: A specific type of storm causes a humanoid's superstition to take effect. Storms can be dust, wind, rain, thunder, lightning, ice, sand, hail, snow, etc.

Sun: Fear of the sun's rays, of bright sunlight, of clouds obscuring the sun's good rays.

Supernatural Beings: A particular kind of supernatural being (or even a specific supernatural being) inspires either a positive or negative superstition.

Undead: Either undead in general or a particular type of undead creature causes this superstition to manifest.

Visions: A specific vision, which comes to a humanoid while he is awake, inspires good luck or bad when it manifests. Visions can be any image, and either frightening or positive in nature.

Weapon: A specific type of weapon frightens or inspires the humanoid if it is being wielded by his opponent.

Wilderness: A specific wilderness type scares or inspires a humanoid. Types include deserts, forests, jungles, swamps, arctic wastes, etc.

Humanoids make use of whatever equipment, arms, and armor they can get their hands on. Many of the races are natural scavengers, picking up anything they can carry and wield. Humanoid characters are subject to class restrictions on weapons.

Armor Restrictions

Normal armor is often hard to fit upon humanoids. While man-sized (M) humanoids can wear human-made armor, those of other sizes or peculiar body shapes, like centaurs, must wear specially-fitted armor or armor of their own race's construction. While human or demihuman armorers can build custom-fitted armor for a humanoid, time is doubled and costs are tripled.

Weapon Breakage (Optional)

Humanoids wielding weapons of their own make need not check for breakage. When large-sized humanoids use human or demihuman weapons, the weapon may break under their greater strength and force. This chance is read directly from the attack roll. Use Table 6 to determine if the weapon breaks. *Weapon Size* refers to the weapon's size classification. *Roll* is the number or less on the 1d20 attack roll that will break the weapon (excluding strength adjustments). A broken weapon becomes useless immediately upon breaking. A magical weapon receives a saving throw vs. crushing blow to avoid breaking.

Table 6: Optional Weapon Breakage

Weapon Size	Roll
S	10
M	5
L	2

Weapon Size Restrictions

Humanoids of large (L) size generally use weapons which also fit into this category. They cannot use tiny weapons (T), at all. They may have trouble wielding small and medium weapons (the DM can assess a –1 to –4 penalty to hit and damage rolls). Some humanoids have bonuses when using weapons of their own make (see the individual entries in Chapter Two).

Likewise, humanoids falling under the tiny (T) size classifications cannot use large weapons (L). They can wield melee weapons of medium size (M) in both hands.

Close-quarter Weapons

Close-quarter weapons are used by those who specialize in close-quarter fighting or who regularly operate in small, enclosed areas, such as underground tunnels. While, in fact, all underground-dwelling humanoids can use these weapons, they are preferred by members of the mine rowdy and tunnel rat kits. Other humanoids with the close-quarter fighting proficiency can also select from these weapons (as long as the weapon in question does not violate the restrictions of a class regarding weapon choice). Humanoids who are not subterranean-dwelling cannot choose these weapons initially, but may gain proficiency with them over the course of a campaign. To use a specific close-quarter weapon, the humanoid must announce its use at the beginning of a combat round. Some of these weapons are also passive, inflicting injury if an opponent gets too close. When used aggressively, Strength bonuses apply.

Body spikes: These are short blades fitted to a humanoid's armor. An opponent who grabs, grapples, or wrestles with a humanoid wearing body spikes from the spikes each round. Body spikes can be used aggressively if the wearer runs at his opponent. The damage inflicted by body spikes depends on the size of

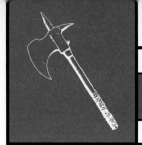

the wearer: T/S = 1d2, M = 1d3, L = 1d4. The spikes are permanently fitted to the armor and cannot be retracted. Spiked armor costs 150% of the normal armor cost.

Kick-slashers: These are crude blades attached to boots or other footwear. The kick-slasher slices into opponents when the user lashes out with his feet. They are not retractable.

Punch-cutter: This is a crude blade attached to open-finger leather gloves. The blade rests on top of the hand, protruding above the knuckles when the fist is closed. When the wearer throws a punch, the punch-cutter slices into his opponent.

Special Humanoid Weapons

Most weapons made or used by humanoids can be found in the *Player's Handbook*. For example, a goblin-made short sword is still a short sword. What follows are rare and unusual weapons rarely found outside of humanoid cultures:

Club, great: This may be a long cudgel lovingly carved from a finely-worked length of oak, or a crudely fashioned bludgeon. Its effects are identical to those of a morning star, though it may be blunt or spiked. Races using these include bugbears, centaurs, and advanced lizard men.

Dart, lizard man: This is a crude, heavy throwing dart that is both fletched and barbed. Measuring two to three feet long, it is used by advanced lizard men. It has a range of 30 yards, and is invariably hurled just before a charge.

Flindbar: A flindbar is a pair of chain-linked iron bars. In combat, the bars are spun around at great speed, striking up to twice in a round. In addition, flindbars can be used to disarm opponents. Each successful hit requires the victim to save vs. wands. If the saving throw is failed, the victim's weapon becomes entangled in the chain and is torn from his grasp. Flind-

bars are made and used by flinds.

Goblin Stick: A goblin stick is a forked and hooked pole arm, used first by bugbears trying to catch the smaller goblins. The goblin stick is a wooden staff, six to nine feet long, gripped in the middle. Each end is tipped with three wicked blades. One hooked blade is used to extract hiding creatures. The other blades are pointed, sharp, and set at slightly different angles to poke into the hardest to reach locations. Goblin sticks are made and used by hobgoblins, bugbears, and ogres.

Lance, flight: This lance has a 10-foot long shaft of tough wood with a sharp stone head, and fletched ends. It is used by flying humanoids as a shock or impact weapon. The flight lance is hurled at the end of a swooping attack and can impale the target.

Giant-kin weapons: Giant-kin weapons, crafted by giant-kin, match their great size and strength. The most common are clubs, daggers, halberds, maces, two-handed swords, and voadkyn long bows.

When using weapons of their own make, giant-kin and other large humanoids suffer none of the penalties associated with the smaller human weapons. Most giant-sized weapons cause more damage than their human-made counterparts. Voadkyn long bows have ranges 50% greater than human-sized long bows.

Oriental Weapons: Used principally by ogre magi and some hobgoblin tribes, most of these can be treated as the western counterpart. Unusual weapons of note include:

Daikyu: A great long composite bow, about seven feet long. The grip is closer to the low end of the bow, allowing it to be more easily fired from horseback or when kneeling.

Katana: An oriental long sword. If worn with the *wakizashi* (short sword), it marks the wearer as one of high social standing. It's a serious insult for an unprivileged character to wear both blades together.

Naginata: An oriental pole arm much like a

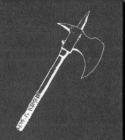

glaive, preferred by female warriors. It has a six to eight foot shaft and swordlike blade.

Tetsubo: A wooden rod about four feet long, the upper half bound with studded iron strips. It is often carried by travelers and can serve as a walking stick. It is typically wielded in two hands.

Pixie weapons: These are weapons that have been scaled down to match pixie and smaller-sized wielders. Unless otherwise noted, their maximum damage is usually in the 1d2 to 1d4 range.

Pixie bow: Resembling tiny short bows of elven design, they have half the range of short bows. Pixies using these have a +4 bonus to their attack rolls. Pixie arrows come in three varieties. *War arrows* inflict damage. *Sleep arrows* render subjects comatose for 1d6 hours if they fail their saving throw vs. spell. *Forget arrows* cause subjects who fail a saving throw vs. spells to suffer a complete loss of memory. Only a clerical *heal* spell or *limited wish* can restore the subject's memory.

Pixie sword: Resembling tiny elven long swords, these are of excellent workmanship. They otherwise perform like daggers.

Saurial Weapons: Saurials weapons perform much as human-made equivalents. Weapons of note include the *bladeback mace,* the *bladeback flail,* and the *hornhead staff.* All saurial weapons are designed for the saurial physiology, having shorter grips, unusual protrusions, and barb-like tips.

Non-saurials trying to use saurial weapons suffer a –1 attack penalty. Likewise, saurials suffer a similar –1 penalty when using non-saurial weapons.

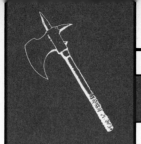

Table 7: Weapons

Item	Cost (gp)	Wgt (lbs)	Size	Type	Speed Factor	Damage S-M	Damage L
Club, great	8	12	M	B	7	2d4	1d6+1
Dart, barbed	*	5	S	P	3	1d4	1d4
Flindbar	8	6	M	B	4	1d4	1d4
Goblin stick	5	8	L	P	7	1d4	1d6
Lance, flight	6	5	L	P	6	1d6+1	2d6

Close-quarter Weapons

Item	Cost (gp)	Wgt (lbs)	Size	Type	Speed Factor	Damage S-M	Damage L
Body spikes	*	*	S	P	2	*	*
Kick-slasher	7**	3	S	S	2	1d4+1	1d6+1
Punch-cutter	6***	1	S	S	2	1d4	1d3

* See entry for information   ** Per foot   *** Per hand

Giant-kin Weapons

Item	Cost (gp)	Wgt (lbs)	Size	Type	Speed Factor	Damage S-M	Damage L
bow, long	125	8	G	—	10	—	—
arrow	1/12	—	G	P	—	1d8	1d8
dagger	5	3	G	P	3	1d6	1d8
halberd	25	35	G	P/S	12	1d12	2d8
mace	11	12	G	B	8	1d8x2	1d6x2
sword, 2-H.	100	35	G	S	13	1d10x2	3d6x2

Oriental Weapons (Ogre Mage)

Item	Cost (gp)	Wgt (lbs)	Size	Type	Speed Factor	Damage S-M	Damage L
Daikyu	100	4	L				
arrow, leaf head	3sp/6	—	L	P	—	1d8	1d6
Katana	100	6	M	S	4	1d10	1d12
Naginata	8	10	L	S	7	1d8	1d10
Tetsubo	2	8	L	B	7	1d8	1d8
Wakizashi	50	3	S	S	4	1d8	1d8

Pixie Weapons

Item	Cost (gp)	Wgt (lbs)	Size	Type	Speed Factor	Damage S-M	Damage L
pixie bow	50	1	T	—	4	Special*	Special*
forget arrow	100/1	—	T	P	—	Special*	Special*
sleep arrow	10/6	—	T	P	—	Special*	Special*
war arrow	1/2	—	T	P	—	1d4+1	1d4+1
pixie sword	30	1	T	S	4	1d4	1d3

* See entry for information

Saurial Weapons

Item	Cost (gp)	Wgt (lbs)	Size	Type	Speed Factor	Damage S-M	Damage L
Bladeback flail	20	25	L	B	9	1d8+1	2d6
Bladeback mace	15	16	L	B	9	1d8+1	1d8
Hornhead staff	5	20	L	B	6	2d6	2d6
Finhead broadsword	17	8	M	S	6	1d8	1d10

Humanoid Size Comparisons

Fremlin Pixie Flyer Kobold Goblin Aarakocra

Beastman Satyr Finhead Bullywug Swanmay Orc Alaghi Mongrelman Half-orc Human

Hobgoblin Flind Wemic Bladeback Lizard Man Bugbear Gnoll Half-orge

Minotaur Centaur Ogre Voadkyn Horn Head Ogre Mage Firbold

Table 9: Humanoid Average Height and Weight

Race	Hgt in Inches Base*	Modifier	Wgt in Pounds Base*	Modifier
Aarakocra	60/58	1d6	80/70	3d10
Alaghi	66/64	1d12	320/290	4d20
Beastman	55/50	1d12	105/85	3d10
Bugbear	72/68	2d10	210/180	6d10
Bullywug	58/56	2d8	125/110	5d10
Centaur	84/80	3d12	1000/960	6d20
Fremlin	12/12	1d6	12/12	2d4
G.kin, firbolg	120/114	1d12	780/740	6d10
G.kin, voadkyn	108/102	1d12	675/650	6d10
Gnoll	84/80	1d12	180/160	4d10
Gnoll, flind	72/69	1d12	165/145	4d10
Goblin	43/41	1d10	72/68	5d4
Hobgoblin	72/68	1d8	150/130	5d10
Human	60/59	2d10	140/100	6d10
Kobold	32/30	3d4	52/48	5d4
Lizard man	60/60	2d12	170/170	3d10
Minotaur	84/80	2d6	450/390	4d20
Mongrelman	60/59	2d12	145/105	4d10
Ogre	96/93	2d12	320/280	3d20
Ogre, half-	84/78	2d6	270/220	6d10
Ogre mage	114/96	2d6	810/780	4d10
Orc	58/56	1d12	130/90	6d10
Orc, half-	60/58	1d12	135/95	6d10
Pixie	24/23	3d6	25/22	4d4
Satyr	55/—	1d10	110/—	4d10
Sr., bladeback	78/76	2d8	550/535	3d20
Sr., finhead	54/52	2d10	150/140	4d10
Sr., flyer	32/30	2d4	65/62	2d12
Sr., hornhead	107/105	2d6	720/700	4d20
Swanmay	—/59	2d10	—/100	6d10
Wemic	78/75	3d6	700/670	4d20

* Females tend to be lighter and shorter than males. Thus, the base numbers for height and weight are divided into male/female values. Note that the modifier still allows for a broad range in each category.

Table 8: Character Kit Summary

Kit	Eligible Class	Eligible Races
Warrior		
Tribal Defender	Fighter	All except fremlin
Pit Fighter	Fighter	All except fremlin
Sellsword	Fighter	All except fremlin
Mine Rowdy	Fighter	Bugbear, gnoll, flind, hobgoblin, minotaur, orc, half-orc, half ogre
Wild. Protector	Ranger*	Beastman, centaur, voadkyn, minotaur, satyr, saurial, swanmay
Paladin, Saurial	Paladin*	Saurial finhead
Wizard		
Hedge Wizard	Any wizard	Centaur, fremlin, voadkyn, minotaur, mongrelman, ogre mage, saurial
Humanoid Scholar	Any wizard	Centaur, fremlin, minotaur, mongrelman, ogre mage, saurial
Outlaw Mage	Any wizard	Centaur, fremlin, voadkyn, minotaur, mongrelman, ogre mage, saurial
Priest		
Shaman	Shaman*	All except beastman, fremlin, minotaur, pixie, satyr, saurial, swanmay
Witch Doctor	W.Doctor*	Bugbear, gnoll, flind, goblin, hobgoblin, kobold, minotaur, half-ogre, orc, half-orc, wemic
Oracle	Cleric, druid	Alaghi, bugbear, centaur, gnoll, flind, goblin, hobgoblin, kobold, mongrelman, half-ogre, orc, half-orc, saurial, swanmay
War Priest	Cleric	Bugbear, gnoll, flind, goblin, hobgoblin, kobold, half-ogre, orc, half-orc, saurial
Wandering Mystic	Any priest	All except aarakocra beastman, bullywug, fremlin, firbolg, voadkyn, lizard man, minotaur, ogre, ogre mage, pixie, satyr, wemic
Rogue		
Scavenger	Any thief	All except alaghi, centaur, firbolg, ogre, half-ogre, saurial, swanmay, wemic
Shadow	Thief	Bugbear, bullywug, gnoll, flind, goblin, hobgoblin, kobold, lizard man, mongrelman, ogre mage, orc, half-orc
Tunnel Rat	Thief	Goblin, hobgoblin, kobold, orc, half-orc
Bard, Humanoid	Bard*	Aarakocra, centaur, flind, mongrelman, satyr, voadkyn, wemic

* A character with this class must take the matching kit.

Table 10: Age

Race	Starting Age Base Age	Variable	Maximum Age Range (Base + Variable)	Average Maximum Age
Aarakocra	15	1d4	50 + 2d12	65
Alaghi	15	1d6	75 + 2d20	95
Beastman	13	1d10	80 + 1d20	90
Bugbear	10	1d6	65 + 2d10	75
Bullywug	10	1d4	60 + 1d20	70
Centaur	18	1d4	75 + 2d20	95
Fremlin	20	1d4	125 + 3d20	155
G.kin, firbolg	40	5d6	200 + 3d100	350
G.kin, voadkyn	75	5d6	250 + 2d100	350
Gnoll	7	1d4	33 + 1d4	35
Gnoll, flind	8	1d6	35 + 1d20	45
Goblin	12	1d6	40 + 1d20	50
Hobgoblin	14	1d6	50 + 1d20	60
Human	15	1d4	90 + 2d20	110
Kobold	12	1d4	95 + 2d20	115
Lizard man	15	1d4	110 + 2d10	120
Minotaur	12	3d6	150 + 1d100	200
Mongrelman	6	1d4	30 + 1d10	35
Ogre	15	1d4	90 + 2d20	110
Ogre, half-	15	1d4	90 + 2d20	110
Ogre mage	20	1d4	175 + 2d20	195
Orc	10	1d4	35 + 1d10	40
Orc, half-	12	1d4	60 + 1d20	70
Pixie	100	5d6	200 + 2d100	300
Satyr	20	3d4	100 + 1d100	150
Sau., bladeback	14	1d12	110 + 1d100	160
Sau., finhead	14	1d12	100 + 1d100	150
Sau., flyer	12	1d10	90 + 1d100	140
Sau., hornhead	14	1d20	125 + 1d100	175
Swanmay	15	1d12	90 + 2d20	100
Wemic	12	1d4	70 + 2d20	90

Table 11: Aging Effects

Race	Middle Age* (1/2 Base Max.)	Old Age** (2/3 Base Max.)	Venerable*** (Base Max.)
Aarakocra	25 years	33 years	50 years
Alaghi	37 years	50 years	75 years
Beastman	40 years	53 years	80 years
Bugbear	33 years	44 years	65 years
Bullywug	30 years	40 years	60 years
Centaur	37 years	50 years	75 years
Fremlin	62 years	83 years	125 years
G.kin, firbolg	100 years	133 years	200 years
G.kin, voadkyn	125 years	167 years	250 years
Gnoll	16 years	22 years	33 years
Gnoll, flind	17 years	23 years	35 years
Goblin	20 years	27 years	40 years
Hobgoblin	25 years	33 years	50 years
Human	45 years	60 years	90 years
Kobold	48 years	62 years	95 years
Lizard man	55 years	73 years	110 years
Minotaur	75 years	100 years	150 years
Mongrelman	15 years	20 years	30 years
Ogre	45 years	60 years	90 years
Ogre, half-	45 years	60 years	90 years
Ogre mage	82 years	116 years	175 years
Orc	17 years	23 years	35 years
Orc, half-	30 years	40 years	60 years
Pixie	100 years	133 years	200 years
Satyr	50 years	67 years	100 years
Sr., bladeback	55 years	73 years	110 years
Sr., finhead	50 years	67 years	100 years
Sr., flyer	45 years	60 years	90 years
Sr., hornhead	62 years	83 years	125 years
Swanmay	45 years	60 years	90 years
Wemic	35 years	46 years	70 years*

*–1 Str/Con; +1 Int/Wis
**–2 Str/Dex; –1 Con; +1 Wis
***–1 Str/Dex/Con; +1 Int/Wis

Aging effects do not allow characters to exceed racial maximums.

Table 12: Racial Ability Requirements

Race	Str	Dex	Con	Int	Wis	Cha
Aarakocra	3/16	8/18	6/16	3/18	3/17	3/18
Alaghi	12/19	3/17	12/18	3/16	3/16	3/16
Beastman	6/18^{50}	6/18	6/16	3/18	3/18	3/16
Bugbear	8/18	8/17	8/18	3/16	3/18	3/14
Bullywug	6/18^{75}	4/18	6/18	3/14	3/16	3/14
Centaur	11/18	3/16	11/18	3/16	4/18	3/18
Fremlin	2/11	8/18	4/13	6/18	3/16	3/18
G.kin, firbolg	14/19	8/15	12/18	8/18	8/18	3/14
G.kin, voadkyn	11/18	13/19	8/16	11/17	3/16	3/18
Gnoll	6/18	5/18	5/18	3/14	3/16	3/14
Gnoll, flind	8/18	6/18	6/18	3/16	3/16	3/16
Goblin	4/15	4/17	5/16	3/18	3/18	3/12
Hobgoblin	6/18	6/18	5/18	3/18	3/18	3/14
Kobold	3/16	4/18	4/15	3/17	3/18	3/14
Lizard man	8/18	3/18	6/18	3/17	3/18	3/16
Minotaur	12/20	5/14	12/20	5/14	3/16	3/16
Mongrelman	6/17	6/18	8/18	3/17	3/18	2/8
Ogre	16/20	2/8	14/20	2/8	2/9	2/8
Ogre, half-	14/18	3/12	14/19	3/12	2/12	2/8
Ogre mage	12/18	7/18	8/14	8/17	3/16	2/14
Orc	6/18	3/17	8/18	3/16	3/16	3/12
Orc, half-	6/18	3/17	13/19	3/17	3/14	3/12
Pixie	3/14	8/19	7/16	6/18	3/16	3/18
Satyr	6/18^{75}	8/18	7/18	3/17	3/18	3/17
Sr., bladeback	10/18	3/14	5/18	3/18	7/18	5/18
Sr., finhead	7/18	5/18	3/18	3/18	3/18	3/18
Sr., flyer	3/17	7/19	3/17	3/18	3/18	3/18
Sr., hornhead	12/18	2/12	8/18	7/19	3/18	3/18
Swanmay, ranger	13/18	13/18	14/18	9/18	14/18	9/18
Swanmay, druid	9/18	9/18	12/18	12/18	12/18	15/18
Wemic	11/18	6/17	11/18	3/18	3/18	3/18

Table 14: Thieving Skill Racial Adjustment

Race	PP	OL	F/RT	MS	HS	DN	CW	RL
Aarakocra	—	-10%	—	-5%	—	+15%	—	-5%
Beastman	—	-5%	-5%	+5%	+5%	—	+5%	-5%
Bugbear	-5%	-5%	—	+10%	+10%	+5%	-5%	-10%
Bullywug	—	-5%	—	—	+5%	—	—	-5%
Centaur	—	—	—	-10%	-5%	—	NA	-5%
Fremlin	+10%	—	—	—	+10%	—	—	—
G.kin, voadkyn	-5%	-5%	—	—	+5%	+5%	—	—
Gnoll	-5%	-5%	—	—	+5%	+5%	—	-10%
Gnoll, flind	—	—	—	—	—	—	—	-5%
Goblin	+5%	—	+10%	+5%	+5%	—	-10%	-10%
Hobgoblin	—	+5%	+5%	—	—	—	—	-10%
Kobold	+5%	—	—	+5%	+10%	+10%	-15%	-10%
Lizard Man	-5%	-5%	—	+5%	+5%	+5%	-5%	-5%
Minotaur	-5%	-5%	—	—	+5%	+5%	-15%	-5%
Mongrelman*	+5%	—	—	+5%	+5%	+5%	-5%	-5%
Ogre mage	-5%	—	—	—	—	+5%	-15%	+5%
Orc	-5%	—	—	—	+5%	+5%	+5%	-10%
Orc, half-	-5%	+5%	+5%	—	—	+5%	+5%	-10%
Pixie	+5%	-10%	—	+5%	+10%	+5%	—	—
Satyr	+5%	-5%	—	+5%	+5%	—	-10%	-5%
Sr., bladeback	—	+5%	+5%	-5%	-5%	—	-15%	—
Sr., finhead	+5%	—	—	—	—	+5%	+5%	—
Sr., flyer	+5%	—	—	—	+10%	+5%	+5%	—
Sr., hornhead	-5%	—	—	-10%	-5%	+5%	-20%	+10%

* Add a 5% bonus to any one thief ability.

Table 13: Humanoid Multi-Class Combinations

Race	Multi-Class Combinations*
Aarakocra	fighter/shaman, fighter/thief
Alaghi	fighter/shaman
Beastman	fighter/thief
Bugbear	fighter/shaman, fighter/thief, fighter/cleric, cleric/thief
Bullywug	fighter/shaman, fighter/thief
Centaur	fighter/mage, fighter/thief, ranger/shaman
Fremlin	mage/thief, illusionist/thief
G.kin, firbolg	fighter/shaman
G.kin, voadkyn	fighter/shaman, fighter/thief, fighter/mage, ranger/mage, mage/thief, fighter/mage/thief
Gnoll	fighter/shaman, fighter/thief, fighter/cleric
Gnoll, flind	fighter/shaman, fighter/thief, fighter/cleric
Goblin	fighter/shaman, fighter/thief, fighter/cleric, cleric/thief
Hobgoblin	fighter/shaman, fighter/thief, fighter/cleric
Kobold	fighter/shaman, fighter/thief, fighter/cleric, cleric/thief
Lizard man	fighter/shaman, fighter/thief

Race	Multi-Class Combinations*
Minotaur	fighter/thief, fighter/mage
Mongrelman	fighter/shaman, shaman/thief, mage/thief, cleric/mage, cleric/thief
Ogre	fighter/shaman (allowed if Wisdom is 9+)
Ogre, half-	fighter/shaman, fighter/cleric (allowed if Wisdom is 9+)
Ogre mage	fighter/mage, fighter/shaman, fighter/thief, mage/thief, fighter/mage/thief
Orc	fighter/shaman, fighter/thief, shaman/thief
Orc, half	fighter/shaman, fighter/thief, shaman/thief, fighter/cleric, cleric/thief
Pixie	fighter/thief
Satyr	fighter/thief
Saurial	dual-class characters are possible
Swanmay	none (dual-class not possible)
Wemic	fighter/shaman

* Witchdoctors can be substituted for shamans if the race has witchdoctors. Witchdoctors and shamans will not come from the same community.

Table 15: Reincarnation Table

Wizard d100 Roll	Priest (Druid) d100 Roll	Incarnation
01-03	—	Aarakocra*
04-05	01-02	Alaghi*
—	03-05	Badger
—	06-10	Bear, black
—	11-13	Bear, brown
06	14-15	Beastman*
—	16-18	Boar, wild
07-09	—	Bugbear*
10-11	—	Bullywug*
—	19-21	Centaur*
—	22-23	Dryad
12-16	—	Dwarf
—	24-26	Eagle
17-21	27-29	Elf
—	30-32	Faun/satyr*
—	33-34	Fox
22	35	Fremlin*
23	36	Giant-kin, firbolg*
—	37-38	Giant-kin, voadkyn*
24-27	—	Gnoll*
28-29	—	Gnoll, flind*
30-34	—	Gnome
35-37	—	Goblin*
38-41	—	Half-elf
42-46	—	Halfling
47-48	—	Half-ogre*
49-51	—	Half-orc*
—	39-41	Hawk
52-54	—	Hobgoblin*
55-68	42-55	Human
69-72	—	Kobold*
73-75	—	Lizard man*
—	56-58	Lynx
76	59-60	Minotaur*
77-79	—	Mongrelman*
80-81	—	Ogre*
82	—	Ogre mage*
83-86	—	Orc*
—	61-63	Owl, giant
—	64-65	Owl, talking
—	66-68	Pixie*
—	69	Pseudodragon /faerie dragon
—	70-71	Raccoon
87	—	Sr., bladeback*
88	—	Sr., finhead*
89	—	Sr., flyer*
90	—	Sr., hornhead*
—	72-76	Stag
—	77-78	Swan
—	79-80	Swanmay*
91-93	—	Troll
94-96	81-82	Wemic*
—	83-87	Wolf
—	88-90	Wolverine
97-00	91-00	DM's choice

* Humanoid races available as PCs in this book.

Table 1: Humanoid Level Limits

Race	Character Group			
	Wr	Wz	Pr	Rg
Aarakocra	11	—	7	11
Alaghi	12	—	11	—
Beastman	12	—	—	10
Bugbear	12	—	8	9
Bullywug	10	—	7	9
Centaur	12	12	14	12
Fremlin	—	10	—	11
Giant-kin, firbolg	12	—	7	—
Giant-kin, voadkyn	11	8	7	10
Gnoll	11	—	9	11
Gnoll, flind	12	—	9	11
Goblin	10	—	9	12
Hobgoblin	11	—	9	11
Kobold	8	—	9	12
Lizard man	12	—	7	9
Minotaur	12	8	7	10
Mongrelman	10	10	10	12
Ogre	12	—	3	—
Ogre, half-	12*	—	4	—
Ogre mage	9	8	7	8
Orc	10	—	9	11
Orc, half-	10*	—	4	8
Pixie	7	—	—	12
Satyr	11	—	—	11
Sr., bladeback	9	9	U	9
Sr., finback	U	9	9	9
Sr., flyer	9	9	9	U
Sr., hornhead	9	U	9	9
Swanmay	14	—	12	—
Wemic	12	—	7	10

* See Table 2.

Table 2: Bonus Levels for Single-Classed Humanoids

Prime Requisite Score	Total Bonus Levels
Racial Maximum +1	+1 (+1)
Racial Maximum +2	+2 (+4)
Racial Maximum +3+	+3 (+7)

Use the parenthetical number if the prime requisite is Strength and if the humanoid is a human crossbreed (half-ogre, half-orc).

Table 16: Monstrous Traits

D100 Roll	Trait
01-05	Bestial Odor
06-09	Bestial Rage
10-12	Monstrous Appearance 1
13-15	Monstrous Strength 1
16-19	Bestial Appetite 1
20-22	Bestial Thirst 1
23-26	Bestial Intelligence 1
27-30	Monstrous Dexterity 1
31-36	Light Sensitivity
37-39	Monstrous Sight
40-42	Monstrous Hearing
43-46	Monstrous Touch
47-50	Monstrous Smell
51-53	Monstrous Taste
54-56	Monstrous Appearance 2
57-58	Monstrous Strength 2
59-61	Bestial Appetite 2
62-64	Bestial Thirst 2
65-67	Bestial Intelligence 2
68-69	Monstrous Dexterity 2
70-72	Bestial Fear
73-80	Bestial Habit (roll on Habit Table)
81-84	Bestial Speech
85-87	Monstrous Craving
88-90	Monstrous Size
91-92	Monstrous Appearance 3
93	Monstrous Strength 3
94	Bestial Appetite 3
95	Bestial Thirst 3
96	Bestial Intelligence 3
97	Monstrous Dexterity 3
98-00	DM's Choice

Bestial Habits

D20 Roll	Beastial Habit
01	Avaricious
02	Brooding
03	Cheat
04	Cowardly
05	Cruel
06	Destructive
07	Drunkard
08	Egoist
09	Feral
10	Filthy
11	Greedy
12	Lazy
13	Liar
14	Miserly
15	Rude
16	Suspicious
17	Thief
18	Violent
19	Whiner
20	DM's Choice

Table 18: General Superstitions

D100 Roll	Superstition
01-03	Air
04-05	Animal/Insect
06-07	Armor
08-09	Being Alone
10	Blood
11-12	Bright Light
13-14	Civilization
15	Clouds
16-17	Cold
18-19	Color
20-21	Darkness
22-23	Day
24-25	Demihumans
26	Destiny
27-28	Dreams
29-31	Earth
32-33	Enclosed Spaces
34-35	Evil/Good/Neutral
36-37	Females/Males
38-40	Fire
41	Flying
42	Future
43-44	Gods
45-46	Heat
47-48	Heights
49-50	Humanoids
51-52	Humans
53-56	Magic
57	Magical Item
58-59	Mobs
60-61	Modern Technology
62-63	Monster
64	Moon
65-66	Night
67-68	Noise
69-70	Open Spaces
71-72	Plants
73	Priests
74	Reptiles
75	Rogues
76-77	Sickness
78-80	Specific Location
81	Stars
82-83	Storms
84	Sun
85	Supernatural Being
86	Touch
87-88	Undead
89	Visions
90	Warriors
91-93	Water
94-95	Weakness
96-97	Weapon
98	Wilderness
99	Wizards
100	DM's Choice

Table 19: Campaign Complications

D20 Roll	Wilderness Complications
01-02	Trait
03-04	Superstition
05-07	Monster
08-10	Humanoids
11-12	Wizard/Cleric
13-14	Warrior/Rogue
15	Adventurers
16-17	Travelers
18-19	Hunters
20	DM's Choice

D100 Roll	Civilization Complications
01-06	Trait
07-12	Superstition
13	Humanoids
14-17	Wizard
18-23	Cleric
24-28	Warrior
29-35	Rogue
36-40	Adventurers
41-42	Travelers
43-45	Hunters
46-49	Mob
50-55	Local Authorities
56-59	Restrictions
60-63	Prejudice
64-68	Fear
69-71	Exploitation
72-75	Captured
76-79	Arrested
80-82	Banished
83-86	Challenged
87-89	Slavers
90-93	Physical Limitation
94-95	Educational Limitation
96-98	Social Blunder
99	Sentenced to Death
00	DM's Choice

Humanoid Character Kit Design Sheet

Character Class: _____

Campaign: _____

Player: _____

Dungeon Master: _____

OVERVIEW:

REQUIREMENTS: _____

ROLE: _____

WEAPON PROFICIENCIES

Required: _____

Recommended: _____

NONWEAPON PROFICIENCIES

Bonus Proficiencies: _____

Required Proficiencies: _____

Recommended, General: _____

Recommended, Warrior: _____

Recommended, Priest: _____

Recommended, Wizard: _____

Recommended, Rogue: _____

Forbidden: _____

EQUIPMENT: _____

_____

SPECIAL BENEFITS: _____

_____

MAGICAL ABILITIES

Major Access: _____

Minor Access: _____

Forbidden Spheres: _____

SPECIAL HINDRANCES: _____

_____

WEALTH OPTIONS: _____

THIEF SKILL BONUSES/PENALTIES

Pick Pockets: _____	Hide in Shadows: _____
Open Locks: _____	Detect Noise: _____
Find/Remove Traps: _____	Climb Walls: _____
Move Silently: _____	Read Languages: _____

Character _____ **HUMANOID WARRIOR**

Alignment_____ Race _____

Class _____ Level _____

Player's Name _____ Clan _____ Religion_____

Sex _____ Age_____ Ht. _____ Kit _____

Wt. _____ Hair _____ Eyes _____

Appearance _____

ABILITIES

STR	Hit Prob	Dmg Adj	Wgt Allow	Max Press	Op Drs	B B/ L G
DEX	Rctn Adj		Missle Att Adj		Def Adj	
CON	HP Adj	Sys Shk	Res Sur		Pois Save	Regen
INT	No of Lang	Spell Lvl	Lrn Sp		Spells/ Level	Spell Immun
WIS	Mag Def Adjus	Bonus Spells		Spell Fail		Spell Immun
CHR	Max No Hench		Loy Base		Rctn Adj	

MOVEMENT

Base Rate [ ]

Light ( )
Mod ( )
Hvy ( )
Svr ( )
Jog (×2)
Run (×3)
Run (×4)
Run (x5)

SAVING THROWS

_____ Paralyze Poison

_____ Rod, Staff or wand

_____ Petrify Polymorph _____

_____ Breath Weapon

_____ Spells _____
Modifier   Save

ARMOR

AC

Adjusted AC   Armor Type (Pieces)

Surprised _____ _____

Shieldless _____ _____

Rear _____ _____

Natural AC _____ _____

Defenses _____

HIT POINTS   Wounds

WEAPON COMBAT

Weapon	#AT	Attack Adj/Dmg Adj	THAC0	Dam (SM/L)	Range	Weight	Size	Type	Speed
				/					
				/					
				/					
				/					
				/					

Special Attacks _____

Ammunition_____ _____ ☐☐☐☐
☐ ☐ ☐ ☐ ☐   ☐ ☐ ☐ ☐ ☐   _____ ☐☐☐☐
☐ ☐ ☐ ☐ ☐   ☐ ☐ ☐ ☐ ☐   _____ ☐☐☐☐

Racial Abilities/Superstitions

_____ _____

_____ _____

_____ _____

_____ _____

_____ _____

_____ _____

_____ _____

Traits_____ _____

_____ _____

_____ _____

Proficiencies/Skills/Languages

(/)   (/)
(/)   (/)
(/)   (/)
(/)   (/)
(/)   (/)
(/)   (/)
(/)   (/)
(/)   (/)
(/)   (/)
(/)   (/)
(/)   (/)
(/)   (/)
(/)   (/)
(/)   (/)

**Kit Benefits
and Hindrances** _____

HUMANOID WIZARD

Character _____

Alignment _____ Race _____

Class _____ Level _____

Player's Name _____ Clan _____ Religion _____

Sex _____ Age _____ Ht. _____ Kit _____

Wt. _____ Hair _____ Eyes _____

Appearance _____

ABILITIES

STR	Hit Prob	Dmg Adj	Wgt Allow	Max Press	Op Drs	B B/ L G
DEX	Rctn Adj		Missle Att Adj		Def Adj	
CON	HP Adj	Sys Shk	Res Sur	Pois Save		Regen
INT	No of Lang	Spell Lvl	Lrn Sp	Spells/ Level	Spell Immun	
WIS	Mag Def Adjus	Bonus Spells		Spell Fail		Spell Immun
CHR	Max No Hench		Loy Base		Rctn Adj	

MOVEMENT

Base Rate [   ]

Light ( )
Mod ( )
Hvy ( )
Svr ( )
Jog (×2)
Run (×3)
Run (×4)
Run (x5)

SAVING THROWS

_____ Paralyze
Poison

_____ Rod, Staff
or wand

_____ Petrify
Polymorph

_____ Breath
Weapon

_____ Spells _____
Modifier   Save

ARMOR

(AC shield)
AC

Adjusted AC   Armor Type (Pieces)

Surprised _____ _____

Shieldless _____ _____

Rear _____ _____

Natural AC _____ _____

Defenses _____

HIT POINTS | Wounds

WEAPON COMBAT

Weapon	#AT	Attack Adj/Dmg Adj	THAC0	Dam (SM/L)	Range	Weight	Size	Type	Speed
				/					
				/					
				/					
				/					
				/					

Special Attacks _____

Ammunition _____ _____ ☐☐☐☐
☐ ☐ ☐ ☐   ☐ ☐ ☐ ☐ _____ ☐☐☐☐
☐ ☐ ☐ ☐   ☐ ☐ ☐ ☐ _____ ☐☐☐☐

Racial Abilities/Superstitions   Wizard Abilities   Proficiencies/Skills/Languages

_____ _____ _____ (/)   _____ (/)
_____ _____ _____ (/)   _____ (/)
_____ _____ _____ (/)   _____ (/)
_____ _____ _____ (/)   _____ (/)
_____ _____ _____ (/)   _____ (/)
_____ _____ _____ (/)   _____ (/)
_____ _____ _____ (/)   _____ (/)
_____ _____ _____ (/)   _____ (/)

Traits _____ _____ _____ (/)   _____ (/)
_____ _____ _____ (/)   _____ (/)
_____ _____ _____ (/)   _____ (/)
_____ _____ _____ (/)   _____ (/)
_____ _____ _____ (/)   _____ (/)
_____ _____ _____ (/)   _____ (/)

Kit Benefits
and Hindrances _____

HUMANOID PRIEST

Character _____

Alignment_____ Race _____

Class _____ Level _____

Player's Name _____ Clan _____ Religion_____

Sex _____ Age_____ Ht. _____ Kit _____

Wt. _____ Hair _____ Eyes _____

Appearance _____

ABILITIES

		Hit Prob	Dmg Adj	Wgt Allow	Max Press	Op Drs	B B/ L G
	STR						
	DEX	Rctn Adj		Missle Att Adj		Def Adj	
	CON	HP Adj	Sys Shk	Res Sur	Pois Save	Regen	
	INT	No of Lang	Spell Lvl	Lrn Sp	Spells/ Level	Spell Immun	
	WIS	Mag Def Adjus	Bonus Spells	Spell Fail	Spell Immun		
	CHR	Max No Hench	Loy Base	Rctn Adj			

MOVEMENT

Base Rate	[ ]
Light	( )
Mod	( )
Hvy	( )
Svr	( )
Jog	(×2)
Run	(×3)
Run	(×4)
Run	(x5)

SAVING THROWS

_____ Paralyze Poison

_____ Rod, Staff or wand

_____ Petrify Polymorph _____

_____ Breath Weapon

_____ Spells _____

Modifier   Save

ARMOR

AC

Adjusted AC   Armor Type (Pieces)

Surprised _____   _____

Shieldless_____   _____

Rear _____   _____

Natural AC _____   _____

Defenses _____

HIT POINTS   Wounds

WEAPON COMBAT

Weapon	#AT	Attack Adj/Dmg Adj	THAC0	Dam (SM/L)	Range	Weight	Size	Type	Speed
				/					
				/					
				/					
				/					
				/					

Special Attacks _____

_____

Ammunition_____ _____ ☐☐☐☐

☐ ☐ ☐ ☐ ☐   ☐ ☐ ☐ ☐ ☐ _____ ☐☐☐☐

☐ ☐ ☐ ☐ ☐   ☐ ☐ ☐ ☐ ☐ _____ ☐☐☐☐

Racial Abilities/Superstitions   Priest Abilities   Proficiencies/Skills/Languages

_____   Turn Undead:_____   (/) _____ (/)

_____   Skeleton/1HD:_____   (/) _____ (/)

_____   Zombie:_____   (/) _____ (/)

_____   Ghoul/2HD:_____   (/) _____ (/)

_____   Shadow/3-4HD:_____   (/) _____ (/)

_____   Wight/5HD: _____   (/) _____ (/)

_____   Ghast:_____   (/) _____ (/)

_____   Wraith/6HD:_____   (/) _____ (/)

Traits_____   Mummy/7HD:_____   (/) _____ (/)

_____   Spectre/8HD:_____   (/) _____ (/)

_____   Vampire/9HD:_____   (/) _____ (/)

_____   Ghost/10HD:_____   (/) _____ (/)

_____   Lich/11+HD:_____   (/) _____ (/)

_____   Special:_____   (/) _____ (/)

Kit Benefits and Hindrances _____

Character _____   **HUMANOID ROGUE**

Alignment _____   Race _____
Class _____   Level _____
Player's Name _____   Clan _____ Religion _____
Sex _____ Age _____ Ht. _____ Kit _____
Wt. _____ Hair _____ Eyes _____
Appearance _____

ABILITIES

	Hit Prob	Dmg Adj	Wgt Allow	Max Press	Op Drs	B B/ L G
STR						
DEX	Rctn Adj		Missle Att Adj		Def Adj	
CON	HP Adj	Sys Shk	Res Sur	Pois Save	Regen	
INT	No of Lang	Spell Lvl	Lrn Sp	Spells/ Level	Spell Immun	
WIS	Mag Def Adjus	Bonus Spells	Spell Fail	Spell Immun		
CHR	Max No Hench		Loy Base		Rctn Adj	

MOVEMENT

Base Rate [   ]
Light ( )
Mod ( )
Hvy ( )
Svr ( )
Jog (×2)
Run (×3)
Run (×4)
Run (x5)

SAVING THROWS

____ Paralyze
Poison ____
____ Rod, Staff or wand
____ Petrify
Polymorph ____
____ Breath Weapon
____ Spells ____
Modifier   Save

ARMOR

AC

Adjusted AC   Armor Type (Pieces)
Surprised _____ _____
Shieldless _____ _____
Rear _____ _____
Natural AC _____ _____

Defenses _____

HIT POINTS   Wounds

———— WEAPON COMBAT ————

Weapon	#AT	Attack Adj/Dmg Adj	THAC0	Dam (SM/L)	Range	Weight	Size	Type	Speed
				/					
				/					
				/					
				/					
				/					

Special Attacks _____
_____
_____

Ammunition _____   ☐☐☐☐
☐ ☐ ☐ ☐ ☐   ☐ ☐ ☐ ☐ ☐ _____   ☐☐☐☐
☐ ☐ ☐ ☐ ☐   ☐ ☐ ☐ ☐ ☐ _____   ☐☐☐☐

Racial Abilities/Traits   Rogue Abilities   Proficiencies/Skills/Languages

Pick pockets: _____
Open locks: _____
Find/remove traps: _____
Move silently: _____
Hide in shadows: _____
Detect noise: _____
Climb walls: _____
Read languages: _____
Traits _____
Backstab: _____

(/)   (/)
(/)   (/)
(/)   (/)
(/)   (/)
(/)   (/)
(/)   (/)
(/)   (/)
(/)   (/)
(/)   (/)
(/)   (/)
(/)   (/)
(/)   (/)

Kit Benefits and Hindrances _____

Gear

Item	Location	Wt.	Item	Location	Wt.	Item	Location	Wt.

Supplies
Water/Wine
☐☐☐☐☐ ☐☐☐☐☐
☐☐☐☐☐ ☐☐☐☐☐

Rations
☐☐☐☐☐ ☐☐☐☐☐
☐☐☐☐☐ ☐☐☐☐☐
☐☐☐☐☐ ☐☐☐☐☐
☐☐☐☐☐ ☐☐☐☐☐
☐☐☐☐☐ ☐☐☐☐☐

Feed
☐☐☐☐☐ ☐☐☐☐☐
☐☐☐☐☐ ☐☐☐☐☐
☐☐☐☐☐ ☐☐☐☐☐

Experience

Treasure

Coins

Gems

Other Valuables

Miscellaneous Information

(Magical Items, Command Words, Small Maps, etc.)

Spell book or Spheres

Henchmen/Animal Companions

Advanced Dungeons & Dragons® Game

The Official DUNGEON MASTER DECKS™

A new way to play... INSTANT ENCOUNTERS!

Introducing the **Deck of Encounters, Set 1** ... featuring more than 400 unique encounters with monsters, magical devices, and nonplayer characters at the flip of a card! Instantly, all the information that you use to create quick, fast-paced, and well-thought-out encounters appears in the palm of your hand. *Deck of Encounters, Set 1*, part of the Official DUNGEON MASTER DECKS™ Series, is for all AD&D® campaigns. Available now at book, game, and hobby stores everywhere!

TSR #9407
Sug. Retail Price
$20.00;
CAN $28.00;
£14.99 U.K.
Incl. VAT
ISBN 1-56076-900-9

New From TSR!